Heartland™
Darkest Hour

Another blinding flash of lightning sent a blue-white glow over their faces. The thunder, when it followed, seemed to turn into a long growl – a growl that grew and became more persistent.

"What's that?" asked Lou, getting off the phone with Scott.

They all craned their ears. The wind outside seemed to build itself into an even greater fury, and Amy heard branches and debris landing on the roof. The growl outside grew louder. It sounded like a speeding train getting nearer.

Grandpa was suddenly all action. "Everyone into the basement," he instructed. "Now! It's a tornado!"

Read all the books about Heartland:

And look out for…

Heartland™

Darkest Hour

Lauren Brooke

With special thanks to Gill Harvey

Scholastic Children's Books,
Commonwealth House, 1–19 New Oxford Street,
London WC1A 1NU, UK
a division of Scholastic Ltd

London ~ New York ~ Toronto ~ Sydney ~ Auckland
Mexico City ~ New Delhi ~ Hong Kong

First published in the UK by Scholastic Ltd, 2003
Series created by Working Partners Ltd

Copyright © Working Partners Ltd, 2003

Heartland is a trademark of Working Partners Ltd.

ISBN 0 439 96866 6

Printed and bound by Nørhaven Paperback, Denmark

4 6 8 10 9 7 5 3

Chapter One

A shrill, excited whinny rang out across the yard. It was followed by the clatter of hooves as a high-spirited chestnut barged out of the horse trailer.

"Hey! Steady, Red." Ben Stillman, one of the Heartland stable hands, struggled to control the powerful gelding. "Take it easy, boy!"

Red gave another high-pitched whinny, calling to his friends in the paddock, and pranced around with his neck arched and his tail held high.

"Here, let me help!" called Amy, jogging over. "He's totally wired."

"Yeah. You'd never think he'd jumped two courses today!" agreed Ben, a cheerful grin on his face as he clung to Red's halter. "Plus the warm-up rounds."

Amy smiled and went to hold the other side of the halter. She spoke to the horse soothingly and stroked his muscular neck. "Let me guess. You won," she said as Red began to calm down.

"How can you tell?" asked Ben, his grin growing wider.

"It's obvious!"

Ben laughed. "Yeah. We won," he said. "Red is jumping out of his skin right now. And boy, doesn't he know it! He's full of himself."

Red was Ben's own horse, a talented showjumper, and the pair were progressing fast in Intermediate classes. Ben was a gifted rider and very ambitious – he and Red made a great team. They had every chance of going far.

Amy tried to stay focused and shut out her feelings as Ben described the details of their winning jump-off. *This could be me*, whispered a voice inside her head. *I could be going to shows and bringing home ribbons, just like Ben.* It was only two weeks ago that she had given up her own show horse, Storm, so that she could concentrate on her real work at Heartland: helping horses with problems to overcome their fear, pain, or distress. Storm was generous and talented, with a great show-jumping career ahead of him, and it had been an agonizing decision for Amy to let him go. She knew Storm had competed at the same show as Red and Ben, and she wondered how he had done.

But Amy pushed those thoughts away. She had done the right thing, she knew that, even though she missed Storm horribly. She helped Ben lead Red to his stall as he continued to whinny greetings to the other horses on the yard.

"I'll give him a good groom," said Ben. "He deserves plenty of pampering."

"It'll calm him down, too," agreed Amy, patting Red, who was sweating slightly with excitement. "I'll see you later."

Amy headed out on to the yard and down the path that led to the paddocks. It was good to see Ben so happy and doing so well. With a pang, she remembered what it felt like to drive home with a blue ribbon on the dashboard. But as she leaned over the paddock gate, she quickly forgot about winning competitions. A young bay pony had lifted her head from grazing and was watching her approach.

Amy let herself into the paddock and called to the pony almost in a whisper, "Willow."

The pony nickered a greeting and began to walk towards her. Amy felt a rush of delight. Willow was barely recognizable as the terrified, bullied pony that had arrived at Heartland only a few weeks earlier, a pony that had been traumatized by old-fashioned breaking methods. She had been tied to a post and hit with sacks, a cruel technique devised to crush a horse's spirit. It made Amy shudder just to think of it. But helping ponies like Willow to forget their pain was the most wonderfully satisfying work in the whole world. Amy couldn't imagine doing anything else.

She held out her hand for the pony to sniff. As she did so, an energetic yearling bounded up and jostled Willow out of the way.

Amy laughed. "Hi, Solly," she said affectionately. "You want your share of attention, too, don't you, boy?"

She patted Solly's neck, then delved into her pocket and fished out some mints for the two horses. Although Solly was younger and far more exuberant than Willow, they were the best of friends.

Quickly, Amy slipped a halter over Willow's head and opened the gate. As she guided the pony out and shut the gate, Solly whinnied in protest and cantered up and down the fence.

"Don't worry, silly," Amy called to him. "You'll have your friend back soon."

Amy took Willow to one of the training rings and tied the lead-rope loosely to the fence. She began to stroke the pony's neck, allowing her hand to travel down over her back. Willow remained relaxed and happy.

"Good girl," whispered Amy. She continued to stroke Willow's back, making sure that the pony showed no signs of anxiety or distress. Willow looked around enquiringly but stood quietly, her ears pricked.

Then Amy gently put her whole arm over the pony's back and leaned, gently at first and then more heavily, so that Willow was supporting most of her weight. Again, the pony seemed content and simply flicked an ear back and forth in curiosity. Amy smiled to herself. She had been building up to this moment all week, and now she was sure that Willow was ready. Very carefully, she lifted herself off the ground with her arms so that her full weight was on Willow. Then, slowly, she swung her leg over the pony's back.

Willow didn't move. Amy sat quietly, her heart fizzing. She patted the pony gently. Just as carefully, she swung her leg back over again and jumped to the ground.

"Good girl, Willow!" she exclaimed, hugging the pony in delight. "That was your big breakthrough. You are such a star!"

"She sure is," said a voice behind her.

Amy turned as Ty, the head stable hand and her boyfriend, approached the gate. "Did you see that?" she asked, smiling at him.

Ty nodded. "It was amazing. She's so calm now. I think she'd do anything for you," he said as the pony reached to sniff at him with her soft muzzle.

"It's not just with me. Look at her," Amy responded as Willow butted Ty with her head. "She's getting more confident every day, with everyone."

She untied Willow and led her to the training ring gate. As she opened it, the pony nudged at Ty's pockets with her probing upper lip. Amy smiled up at Ty, and their eyes met. Gently, he bent down and kissed Amy on the forehead.

"Another happy horse," he said softly. "And all thanks to you. You're pretty incredible." Then he straightened up. "I'd better get going. I was going to bring in Dylan and Candy from the far paddock so we can turn some ponies out."

"I'll come with you," said Amy. "I'll just take Willow back first."

Together, they walked down to Willow's paddock in the early evening sun. Solly whinnied when he saw his friend and trotted over to greet her as Amy slipped off Willow's halter. The two horses touched noses before wandering off to graze.

Amy and Ty headed to the next paddock. Despite the sweltering daytime heat, the late summer evenings were getting chilly, and some of the finer-bred horses needed to be brought into their stalls overnight.

"I'll get Dylan," said Ty as he made his way towards the big bay showjumper that was grazing with three of the other horses.

Amy shielded her eyes against the sun to look for Candy, a strawberry roan mare that had arrived at Heartland only a few days before. Her owner, Barbara Goldman, had been riding her in dressage classes on a regular basis, but recently the mare had begun to pull at the bit and sidestep for no apparent reason. Mrs Goldman had sent her to Heartland to find out why.

Amy spotted Candy on her own, near the far end of the paddock. She seemed to be dozing, with one hind leg resting. Not wanting to startle the horse, Amy walked over cautiously. Candy turned to look at her but didn't step away.

Amy frowned. Candy usually moved away when they came to catch her – she liked to play a game. She would continually move as she grazed, one eye on the person trying to catch her, putting up a show of not wanting to be caught. But today, Amy walked right up to her and slipped the halter over her head.

"Come on, girl," said Amy. "You're coming in for the night."

She gave a gentle tug on the lead-rope, and Candy stepped forward reluctantly. Amy stopped and looked at her.

"What is it?" called Ty, leading Dylan over.

"I'm not sure," said Amy. "Candy seems … lifeless. Look. Her eyes are kind of dull, and she didn't go through her whole routine when I tried to catch her."

She stroked the mare's neck. The air had a chill in it, but she could feel that Candy was sweating. "I'm sure she has a temperature," she said, worried. "We'd better get her up to the barn and check."

Candy walked to the yard slowly, with Amy and Ty coaxing her every step of the way. Amy settled her into one of the stalls in the back barn, while Ty went to find a thermometer. Amy checked the mare over in case she had a cut that had become infected. But she couldn't find anything. Hopefully, it was just a reaction to the change of environment, but Amy knew that wasn't very likely.

"Here's the thermometer," said Ty, appearing at the stall door. "Could you hold her for me?"

"Sure," said Amy. "But I don't think she's going to react much. She doesn't seem to have any energy at all."

Ty stood by Candy's tail and took her temperature while Amy patted and reassured her. They waited for a minute.

"Whoa!" Ty exclaimed when he saw the reading.

"What is it?" asked Amy anxiously.

"A hundred and four," said Ty. "We'd better call Scott."

Amy nodded, knowing the normal reading for a horse was a hundred and one. "It must be some kind of infection," she said. "Most likely flu or strangles, I guess." She checked the area around Candy's throat, and the horse flinched. "If it's strangles, her lymph nodes would be swollen," she said. "It's definitely tender there, but there's no inflammation. We'll just have to see what Scott says and keep her away from other horses in case it's contagious."

Amy left Ty to finish with Candy and ran to the farmhouse. Lou, Amy's older sister, was just on her way outside when Amy burst through the door.

"Hey! What's up?" she asked as Amy crashed into her.

"I have to call Scott," explained Amy, slightly out of breath. "One of the horses is sick. Candy, the new arrival. We're not sure what it is, but her temperature's sky-high. It might be strangles."

"Is that serious?" asked Lou, who did not work as closely with the horses as Amy did.

"Well, strangles is easy to treat," said Amy. "But it's highly contagious, which is trouble. Anyway, we don't know yet. It could be something else." She reached for the phone and dialled Scott's number. Scott was the local equine vet, who also happened to be Lou's boyfriend.

"Hi, Scott," said Amy when he answered his cellphone. "It's Amy," she added. "How quickly could you come over to Heartland? One of the mares is running a really high temperature. Ty and I are worried it might be strangles or flu."

"I'm at a ranch on the other side of town," said Scott, "but I could be there in a couple of hours. Keep her isolated until I get there. A lot of germs are going around right now."

"Sure," Amy said. "Is there anything else we should do?"

"Just make sure she's warm and comfortable. I'll be there as soon as I can."

"Thanks, Scott."

Amy put the phone down and looked at her sister.

"Is he coming over?" Lou asked.

Amy nodded. "But not for a couple of hours."

Lou studied Amy's anxious face. "This isn't a major problem, is it?" she asked. "You look pretty worried."

Amy relaxed slightly. "I hope not," she said. "Most things are treatable. That's the case with strangles – you just need antibiotics."

"I guess we'll have to wait and see. Let me know when Scott gets here. I'll be grooming Ivy," said Lou. She walked to the door, then paused. "By the way, there was a message on the machine for you. Daniel called," she said, and headed outside.

"Thanks," Amy yelled after her.

Daniel! He must have been calling to let her know how Storm did at the show. The thought of Storm made her smile. Her own horse, the horse she loved so much – the horse she'd had to part with. She had sold him to Nick Halliwell, a local showjumper and trainer. Storm was being cared for by Daniel Lawson, one of Nick's working pupils. Now it was Daniel who fed Storm every day, Daniel who groomed him – and Daniel who rode him in shows.

Amy knew that she couldn't have found Storm a better home. Daniel was her friend, and he loved Storm almost as much as she did. Quickly, she punched in the number of Nick Halliwell's stables.

Daniel himself answered.

"Amy!" he exclaimed as soon as he heard her voice. "Guess what?"

"Did you win?" Amy asked anxiously.

"Yes! Storm went like a dream. It was amazing. He just floated around the course and still beat the next horse by three seconds." Daniel laughed. Amy recognized the tone of his voice, the exhilaration. Storm was a dream horse, and he was even better at shows. She listened as Daniel described their first round and then the jump-off, imagining every moment of it. *If only I'd been there,* she kept thinking.

"I just feel so lucky. I can't thank you enough, Amy," said Daniel. His voice became gentle. "I know you said you want to hear about the shows, but I won't go into all the details if it's too hard."

"It's fine," Amy replied quickly. "I made the right decision, and I'm glad you and Storm are doing so well. You're the right person for him. I appreciate your understanding, anyway."

"Of course I understand," said Daniel. "I know what it's like to give up competing. I mean, I had to stop when I lost Amber."

Amber had been Daniel's own horse, a brave, big-hearted strawberry-roan mare that had to be put down after a show-jumping accident.

"But, Daniel, that was so much worse," said Amy. "It's easier for me. Storm's still alive and doing what he loves best."

"I know, but you chose to give up showing – so you could concentrate on Heartland. And then, when you realized how much Storm missed the show ring, you chose to give him up, too. I know it was for his own good, but I don't think I could have done that. Anyway, I know how much you miss him. You have to come over to see him soon. And to see me, of course."

"I will!" Amy said with a laugh. "You couldn't keep me away! But it may be a while. We're pretty busy here, and we have a sick horse." Quickly, she explained the situation with Candy. "I'll come as soon as I have time," she promised.

Amy put the phone down and went back outside. She hurried to the back barn where Ty was still with Candy. He had put a stable blanket over her back, and he was just sponging her nose. He was looking worried. "She's started to cough," he said. "And her nose is running."

"Poor girl," said Amy, stroking her neck. "She's still sweating. Scott can't get here for a couple of hours. He said just to keep her comfortable – and isolate her in case it's contagious."

Amy and Ty looked at each other. Amy could see that the same thought was running through Ty's mind. *If it's contagious, we have a big problem.* Candy had been out in the fields, grazing with the other horses and using the water trough for several days, and at night she'd been in the confined space of the barn, where diseases spread more easily. Some of the other horses might already be infected – or one of them might have given Candy the infection in the first place.

"At least we're up to date with all our vaccines," said Amy. "It can't be anything too serious. I'll put some echinacea in her feed to help boost her immune system."

"Good idea," agreed Ty. "We'll just have to keep an eye on

her. And one of us needs to make sure none of the other horses has any symptoms. I can go."

"OK," agreed Amy. "I'll give Candy some T-touch to help her relax."

Ty headed out, and Amy turned her attention to the sick horse. Candy stood listlessly, coughing occasionally, as Amy began to massage up and down her neck, working in tiny circles with her fingertips. The mare was quiet but kept shifting restlessly, and Amy could sense that she was suffering.

About half an hour later, Ty put his head around the barn door.

"All the other horses seem OK," he said. "Looks like Candy's the only one who has it, whatever it is. How is she?"

"She's feeling pretty bad, I think," said Amy. "I'll stay with her until Scott gets here."

At last, Amy heard the sound of Scott's pickup in the driveway and ran from the barn to meet him.

"Where is she?" asked Scott, looking concerned.

"She's in the back barn," said Amy. "We've put the other horses in the front barn – the ones we needed to bring in."

"Good," said Scott as they hurried to the barn. "I hope it's not flu. There's a nasty strain of it going around."

Even before they reached the barn, they could hear Candy coughing. It sounded as though her cough was growing steadily deeper. Ty joined them, and they all approached quietly. When they arrived at her stall, the mare was standing dejectedly, and her nose was dripping with clear mucus.

"You took her temperature?" asked Scott, letting himself into the stall.

Ty nodded. "It was a hundred and four."

Swiftly, Scott took it again. "It's still the same," he said. "So it's stable, at least."

He examined her carefully, looking at her eyes and throat and listening to her chest as she coughed. Then he opened his bag and took out a syringe. "We'll need to do some tests," he said, quickly taking a blood sample, "but I'm afraid it's almost certainly equine flu. I've seen a lot of cases of it lately."

"I thought it might be strangles because her throat is tender," said Amy.

"I don't think so," said Scott. "Her cough is pronounced, and she hasn't developed any throat abscesses, which always accompany strangles."

"So that's good news. Because strangles is so contagious, right?" asked Amy.

Scott didn't answer immediately.

"She will be OK, won't she, Scott?" Amy prompted. "The flu's a virus, isn't it?"

Scott ran his hand down the mare's neck. "Yes, it's a virus," he said. "Which means you can't treat it with antibiotics. You just have to let it run its course. Most horses recover after a few days, but their immune systems will be compromised. Especially from running a fever in this heat. It will be important to protect against secondary infections. Complications will be more likely in the old and young horses than in strong adults like Candy."

Amy was relieved. At least things looked good for Candy in the long run. "So what should we do to guard against further infections?" she asked. "I was going to give her some echinacea. Will that help?"

"Yes. That will give her immune system a boost," said Scott. He looked around the barn. "The barn's dry and well ventilated, which is good," he added. "You need to keep her warm with a good blanket and feed her often, but only a little at a time. You should dampen the feed – anything dry and dusty will aggravate her cough."

Amy nodded, then frowned. "But I don't understand. All the horses here are vaccinated against flu," she said. "We make sure they've had a vaccine before they come."

Scott nodded. "The problem is that flu can mutate. There can be several strains, just like the common cold in humans. The vaccine only works against the most common strains. It can't protect against every new mutation, and there seems to be a new strain that is particularly potent."

"The flu is as contagious as strangles, right?" asked Ty. "Can we do anything to keep it from spreading?"

Scott looked at their worried faces. "Keep Candy on her own. I'll check all the other horses for symptoms before I go. Then just keep a close eye on them yourselves."

"I just checked them," said Ty. "They're all OK for now."

"Well, that's something," said Scott. "But if any of them start coughing or running a temperature, separate them right away. And don't take any new horses until you get the all-clear. If it's what I think it is, this flu strain is too strong to mess with."

Amy stared at him. "That means…"

"Yes," said Scott gently. "I'm sorry, but Heartland will have to be isolated."

Chapter Two

"So? What's the news?" demanded Lou anxiously when Amy, Scott and Ty entered the farmhouse.

"Candy has equine flu," said Amy. "And Heartland is under quarantine."

"Well, we can't be one hundred per cent sure yet. We need to see the test results," said Scott. "But flu's the most likely cause of her symptoms. I'm going to need to run through procedures with you all."

They sat down at the kitchen table, and Grandpa joined them from the back room.

"The flu is like strangles in that it spreads like wildfire," said Scott. "So you're going to have to be really careful. Chances are that even vaccinated horses won't be protected against this strain. Anything that Candy has come into contact with should be washed down with a disinfectant – and everything that you've had contact with since handling her," he added, looking at Ty and Amy. "I know it's a pain, but the more you do to contain this, the better."

Amy sighed when she realized what this meant. She and Ty had both handled Candy over the last couple of days. Then they'd cleaned tack, filled the feed buckets and the water buckets, mucked out stalls – the list went on. They had a lot of work to do.

"All the horses currently at Heartland are at risk," Scott continued. "Some may have already contracted the virus. You've got to watch them all for symptoms and isolate them the moment the symptoms develop."

"But will they be OK?" asked Lou. "How long does it last?"

"They should start recovering after five or six days. It's not the flu itself that causes problems – it's what comes afterwards. Young horses, in particular, tend to get secondary infections, like pneumonia, or sometimes a horse develops a chronic cough. The illnesses will hit weakened immune systems hard. You'll have to keep a close watch. Otherwise, just keep the infected horses isolated until there is no more risk of contagion. That takes about three weeks. You're going to have to cancel all your prospective arrivals until I give the all-clear."

Lou looked shocked. She shook her head in disbelief. "Do people have to remain isolated?" she asked anxiously.

"No. But you need to make sure that you scrub down and wear clean clothes when you leave the farm," said Scott. "And set up a boot dip and some overalls for when you're handling

Candy. That way, you'll minimize chances of the germs spreading."

Silence fell around the table as everyone digested the information. Then Scott spoke again. "You're going to have to tell all the owners, obviously," he said. "And for horses that actually contract the flu, you need to emphasize that they won't be able to return to work for several weeks after they've recovered. Having such a high temperature puts a lot of strain on a horse's heart and can cause permanent damage. That's especially important for competition horses."

"What's this about competition horses?" asked Ben cheerily, coming through the door. His expression changed when he saw the solemn faces in front of him.

"Candy's got equine flu," Amy told him. "Or it looks that way. Scott was just telling us what we should do to keep it from spreading."

Ben's face turned pale. "And what were you saying about competition horses? It's not going to affect Red, is it? He's had his vaccine."

"I'm afraid that won't make any difference," said Scott gravely. "The vaccine doesn't cover this strain. If it's what I think it is, you're going to have to quarantine Red for a few weeks, even if he doesn't get the virus himself."

Ben stared at Scott as though he hadn't heard him right. "Quarantine! You mean I won't be able to take him to shows?"

"I'm afraid not," said Scott. "Not until we're sure he's not incubating the virus."

"But how could he be? I can't just cancel everything like that!"

Amy looked at Ben's stricken face, and her heart went out to him. Competing on Red was so important to him, and this season the pair had been working really well together.

"You don't really have much choice, Ben," said Scott. "We can't risk exposing other horses to the virus."

"I can't believe this," Ben muttered angrily. His expression looked almost accusing. "I have back-to-back shows coming up."

"It's no one's fault," said Scott gently. "The flu virus is unpredictable. No owner can protect against new strains. It might be worth trying to find out where Candy caught it, but basically, it's just bad luck."

Ben sighed and ran a hand through his hair. "You can say that again," he replied a little irritably.

Amy was surprised. She knew that this was tough for Ben, but she hadn't imagined he would react this badly. She stood up. "I'm going to call Barbara Goldman," she said. "She needs to know about Candy right away, and I'll ask her where Candy might have contracted the flu."

Amy wasn't looking forward to speaking to Barbara. When Barbara had brought Candy to Heartland, she had found it difficult to admit to Amy that Candy had a problem she couldn't solve. Barbara had trained her since she was a yearling; Candy was now eleven, and a highly disciplined dressage horse. The talented horse had recently taken to playing with the bit and ignoring simple directive cues, a problem Amy thought would be relatively easy to treat. Amy knew that Barbara was hoping to compete on Candy again within a month, but there wasn't a hope of that now.

As Amy expected, Barbara sounded upset and shocked at the news. "But her vaccinations are right up to date!" she exclaimed. "Are you sure it's flu?"

"Well, we can't be certain, yet," said Amy. "But our vet, Scott Trewin, has seen her and says that it's almost certainly equine flu."

"When will you know for sure?" queried Barbara.

"We have to wait for the test results, but Scott says that he's seen a number of cases of this strain of flu lately. Apparently, the vaccination is ineffective against it," said Amy. "Has Candy been to a show recently or come into contact with horses outside your barn?"

"Are you suggesting she had the flu before she arrived at Heartland?" Barbara asked, slightly defensively.

"I'm afraid it's likely," said Amy. "None of our other horses have symptoms."

There was silence on the other end of the line.

"Well," said Barbara eventually, "none of the other horses here are sick, either, but I suppose she might have picked it up at the Blueridge Show. I took her there last weekend." Her tone was almost apologetic now, and Amy found herself feeling sorry for her.

"I'll come to see Candy in the morning," finished Barbara. "I hope you can give her all the care she needs."

"Yes, we can," Amy assured her, mentioning everything they'd already done to comfort the sick horse. She shook her head and sighed as she put the phone down. She turned to Lou. "What a nightmare," she said. "I hate having to give someone bad news."

"And she's just the first," said Lou ruefully. "We'll have to let all the other owners know that their horses are at risk – and that they'll have to pass quarantine before we can let them go."

Amy nodded. "Let's just hope that Candy's our only case," she said. But her heart was heavy. Candy had been grazing with the other horses for days now. If none of them had been infected, it would be little short of a miracle.

The next two days passed in a blur. First of all, Amy and Ty spent a whole day scrubbing and disinfecting the yard, the feed-room, and the tack-room to minimize the chances of spreading the virus. They emptied the water troughs in the paddocks, scrubbed them out, and refilled them. They checked on the horses every few hours to make sure they hadn't developed any symptoms. Amy's hands were raw from disinfectant.

Barbara Goldman arrived, stunned that this had happened to her horse and frustrated that she couldn't simply take Candy away. But Scott confirmed that Candy had the strain of flu he had suspected. There was no other option: Candy had to stay where she was, and Heartland had to remain closed to all other horses.

"How is she?" asked Amy, coming into the back barn with a bran mash for Candy. Ty was taking the mare's temperature again. It had remained high over the past couple of days, her cough had become rougher and more frequent, and she had almost completely lost her appetite. She had only been eating a few mouthfuls of mash each day.

"Well, fingers crossed," said Ty. "I think she's past the worst. Her temperature's down to a hundred and three."

Amy let out a sigh of relief. "And none of the other horses are showing any symptoms," she said. "We might be lucky."

She put the bucket of mash down in front of Candy, who nosed at it without much interest. "Come on, girl." Amy tried to encourage her. "It's got fenugreek in it. You like that." The mash was slightly warm and smooth enough not to hurt the mare's tender throat. The fenugreek would help her breathe more easily, too. Candy halfheartedly took a mouthful and chewed it slowly.

"That's it," Amy said, soothing the mare. She smiled at Ty. "Mrs Goldman will be happy to hear she's on the mend. She really cares for Candy. I could tell when she came to visit."

Ty nodded. "Well, Candy's used to getting a lot of attention, that's obvious enough," he said. He wiped the thermometer and put it back in its container.

"Hey, you two! Can I come in?" called a voice from the door. It was Soraya, Amy's best friend from school.

"Soraya! Wait there," Amy called back. "I'll come to you." As Scott had suggested, they had set up a boot dip and kept extra overalls at the barn door to reduce the risk of carrying the virus around the yard. "I won't be long. I'm just feeding one of the horses."

"You go," said Ty. "I'll stay with Candy and try to get her to eat a little more."

"OK, if you're sure," said Amy. "I wanted to do some work with Willow and Solly afterwards, too."

Amy left Ty in the stall and slipped off her overalls. She disinfected her rubber boots, then hurried out to see Soraya. Soraya was just back from summer camp, and Amy knew she'd want to tell her all about it.

"Hey, Amy!" Soraya cried, giving her friend a hug. "I just saw Lou. She told me about the flu. I'm really sorry."

"Yeah," said Amy. "But we're coping. There's only one case so far. And quarantine only lasts a few weeks. We'll get through it. So how was camp?"

"Great," said Soraya enthusiastically. "But that can wait till later. Right now, I'm here to help. What can I do?"

Amy grinned at her. Soraya was always so good at helping out whenever Heartland needed her. She squeezed her arm. "Why don't you go and find Ben?" she said. "Some of the horses need exercising. Maybe you could convince him to go on a trail ride with you. It might cheer him up."

"Why? Is he down about something?" asked Soraya, whose interest in Ben didn't seem to have waned during her weeks away.

"Red's in quarantine, like all the other horses," explained Amy. "Ben's not dealing with it well. It means he can't compete for a few weeks, and he's been in a foul mood ever since he found out."

"Right," said Soraya understandingly. "That figures. Is it OK to go on the trails, though?"

"Just as long as you avoid Clairdale Ridge. Other horses go that way sometimes. But it'll be fine if you go on the other path around Teak's Hill. You should take Dylan. He needs the exercise, and he's a lot of fun. I guess Ben will ride Red."

"I'll do my best to bring him back smiling," said Soraya, laughing.

"You'd be doing us all a favour!" responded Amy with a smile, and she headed off towardss the paddocks.

Amy was looking forward to working with Solly and Willow. There had been less time to work with the horses since Candy had been sick, and she was feeling frustrated at not being able to do as much as the horses really needed. Solly had been sent to Heartland to learn some stable manners, and he would quickly lapse back into bad behaviour if he didn't get regular attention. Willow needed a follow-up to her backing breakthrough to make sure she continued to grow more comfortable with the idea of having someone on her back. But they weren't the only ones. There was Blackjack, a mature show horse that had been sent to Heartland because he was getting so bad-tempered that he was difficult to groom. Figuring out his problems would take a lot of time and careful observation. And Ivy, who spooked at just about everything. The list went on. But Amy smiled as she saw Soraya approach Dylan's stall. Dylan was Nick Halliwell's young showjumper. He had come to Heartland a gangly, uncoordinated mess. Amy and Ty had put a lot of time into helping the horse become more conscious of his own movement. Their work with him had been a total success, and if it hadn't been for the flu, Nick would have taken him home this week.

Amy reached the paddock gate and looked for Solly and Willow. They were bound to be grazing together. She had a couple of hours – enough time to teach Solly to go through a gate on a lead-rope in a civilized manner and, she hoped, to take the next step with Willow and teach her to walk with a rider on her back.

Amy quickly spotted them, not far from the gate, and her heart sank.

"Willow," she whispered. The bay pony was standing with her head hanging low, not grazing. Solly was nosing at his friend anxiously, sensing that something was wrong.

Amy let herself into the paddock and walked over to the pair. Solly whinnied, but Willow shifted listlessly, barely lifting her head. Amy placed a hand on her neck and felt that she was sweating. As she did so, Willow gave a shallow cough, her breath rasping hoarsely. There couldn't be much doubt: Willow had the virus – and that almost certainly meant Solly would come down with it, too.

Amy sighed. Just when they thought they'd been lucky! She slipped a halter over Willow's head and led her to the gate. Solly followed at their heels, whickering anxiously, not wanting to be left behind.

"Don't worry, I'll be back for you," Amy said to him, shutting him in as she led Willow out of the field. "I'm afraid you're both going to have to come into the barn."

Ty saw her leading Willow up the path and came to meet her. "Don't tell me," he said, running a hand through his hair.

"Yes," said Amy. "Another case. For sure."

"What about Solly?"

"He seems OK at the moment, but I think we'll have to bring him in anyway. He's bound to have the virus, isn't he?"

Ty frowned. "I guess so. But we can't just put him with the infected horses if he doesn't have symptoms. He might be OK, and that would just increase his chances of getting sick."

"And we can't put him in the front pasture because he could infect the horses there," said Amy. "Maybe we should keep him out for now. I could ask Grandpa to section off part of the bottom paddock. It's not ideal, but what else can we do?"

As she spoke, the significance of this new development began to sink in. Apart from the extra work and worry involved in caring for sick horses, a new case meant that the quarantine would have to be extended. Heartland wasn't going to be free of infection as quickly as they'd hoped. She looked at Ty in frustration.

"Hey," he said softly, touching Amy's arm. "It *will* be OK, you know. We can get through this. We've had to deal with worse things."

Amy nodded and smiled. "That's true," she said. "I'd better get Willow inside and find her a blanket," she added as the pony coughed again.

"I'll talk to Jack about the paddock," offered Ty. "You get Willow settled in."

"Thanks, Ty," Amy said, and gently pulled on the horse's lead-rope.

As she led Willow into the stall next to Candy and covered her back with a light blanket, Amy couldn't help thinking of Ben. He was going to be devastated by the news. It was such bad timing, when he and Red had been doing so well. And he was taking it so badly. Amy had given up competing on Storm and knew how it felt to have it suddenly taken away, but competing had never been everything to her, the way it was to Ben. Working with the horses at Heartland was her first concern.

She found herself wondering how Daniel would feel about Ben's situation. Then she realized that she'd barely had time to think of Storm over the past few days. What if the flu had hit Nick Halliwell's stables, too? Certainly, some of his horses had gone to the Blueridge Show. How would she feel if Storm were sick? She knew she'd want to look after him herself – and she wouldn't be able to. She'd just have to trust Daniel to care for him properly. Thinking about it made her realize how difficult it must be for owners like Barbara Goldman, seeing their sick horses being cared for by strangers.

But Daniel wasn't a stranger, he was a good friend. Amy suddenly remembered that she'd promised to visit him as soon as she could. She'd have to find the time, somehow. She resolved to call Daniel later that day. But for now, she had to concentrate on Willow. She took the pony's temperature and found it was a hundred and three. It would probably rise further, and the pony was miserable enough already. Amy frowned. How many more horses were going to be affected? She hardly dared think about it.

But she soon had to. Ty appeared at the barn door, looking grave. He leaned over Willow's door. "I talked to Jack," he said. "He's putting up a temporary fence now, but I'm not sure it's going to help. Think about it. Candy has never been in the same paddock as Willow. So how did Willow get the virus?"

Amy looked at Ty. "Well, I guess there was only a fence between them."

"But if it's passed between the paddocks…" said Ty.

Amy nodded slowly. She knew exactly what he meant. Any horse that had been out in the paddocks over the last week would have been exposed to the virus.

"It's a time bomb," she whispered, and she knew it was just the beginning.

Chapter Three

As Amy and Ty walked up the path together, Ben and Soraya clattered into the yard on Red and Dylan. Ben was looking slightly more cheerful, and Soraya flashed Amy a grin.

"Good ride?" called Amy as they dismounted.

"Pretty good, thanks," replied Soraya. She and Ben ran up their stirrups. "How are things here?"

Amy glanced at Ty and braced herself to break the bad news. She had the feeling that Ben wasn't going to take it too well, but there was nothing she could do about that. "Not great," she admitted as Lou appeared at the feed-room door.

"Why?" asked Lou. "It's not Candy, is it?"

Amy shook her head. "No. Candy's doing OK."

Ben looked up from loosening Red's girth. "Don't tell me," he said. "There's another case of flu."

"Yes," said Amy. "It's Willow this time."

"So the quarantine is going to have to be extended," said Ben in a flat voice.

"For a few more days, yes," agreed Amy awkwardly.

"That's another show I'll miss," said Ben abruptly. "That's great."

To Amy's surprise, Ty turned to Ben angrily. "It's not exactly the end of the world, is it?" he demanded. "So you have to miss a couple of shows. Big deal. We're trying to care for sick horses here. That's what Heartland's about – I'm sure you remember that."

Ben looked taken aback, but he was quick to find a response. "OK, Ty, we all know competing doesn't mean anything to you. Fine. But don't try to tell me how I should feel about it. I've been trying to qualify for the tristate finals all year, and I need just one more first-place finish, but I'm running short of shows. It's hard to see a year's work gone just like that."

"I just wish you'd keep things in perspective," Ty answered. "Red doesn't even have the virus. Now we have two sick horses to look after, and there may be a lot more before all this is over. We need to pull together and get the work done."

Ben's face stiffened. "Well, thanks for sharing your opinion, Ty," he said coldly. "Maybe next time you could try to see someone else's point of view." Abruptly, he lifted the saddle from Red's back and marched off to the tack-room, almost bumping into Jack, who was just returning from the paddocks.

An embarrassed silence fell over the yard, and Amy's

grandfather looked around questioningly. "What's wrong with Ben?" he asked.

"Willow has the flu," explained Amy, "and Ben's upset because it extends the quarantine."

"He's being selfish," Ty burst out. "As if a couple of shows really matter that much."

Amy felt torn. Part of her understood how Ben felt. Missing shows at this stage in the season was important. It would take another couple of shows to get Red back into the swing of things, and he had been so close to qualifying. But Ty was right. The sick horses should be everyone's priority right now.

"Our biggest concern is that Candy and Willow hadn't been in close contact," she said. "So it looks like any of the horses could be infected."

Jack looked concerned. "Well, it's best to be prepared for the worst," he said. "Are there any more measures we can put in place?"

"We've done everything we can to minimize the risk to the other horses," said Ty, who had quickly refocused on the issue at hand. "But Candy must have passed it on while she was still in the paddock."

Amy nodded. "We just have to continue being really careful. Change overalls and dip our boots at the door of the barn, keep anything to do with the sick horses separate. Maybe it would be easier if only Ty and I go into the barn."

"Good idea," said Jack. "There's not much reason for the rest of us to go in there. We'll just have to do everything we can to keep things running smoothly."

* * *

The sound of a car making its way up the driveway brought the impromptu meeting to an end. As it pulled into the yard, Soraya waved at her mother. "I asked Mom to pick me up," said Soraya. "I'd better go."

Amy walked with her to the car. "Sorry we didn't get to catch up more. And it looks like your good work with Ben has just been undone," she commented wryly.

Soraya shook her head and smiled. "No big deal. The ride was good," she said. "Dylan went so well, I couldn't help but have a good time. But Ben is another story. He was really preoccupied. I don't think he'll want to open up to anyone, especially not after that confrontation with Ty."

Amy nodded. "I guess the tension's getting to all of us," she said.

"Well, at least he's got Red. That horse sure means a lot to him," said Soraya, getting into the car. "I'll be over again soon to help. I think you might need it."

Amy waved as she watched the car pull away, thinking about what Soraya had said about Ben and his bond with Red. Amy headed towards the barn, planning to start on the evening feeds. Then she changed her mind and went indoors. She felt she had to check on Storm before doing anything else. She picked up the phone and dialled Nick Halliwell's number.

"Hi, Nick," she said when he answered. "It's Amy."

"Amy," he said. "I hear from Lou that you're having a rough time at Heartland."

"Yes," said Amy. "But Dylan's still healthy, so far. We'll just have to keep him here until we get the all-clear."

"I understand," said Nick. "We had a flu outbreak here a few years back. It's a real nuisance and a lot of work. But I'm sure you're dealing with it as well as you can."

"We're doing our best," said Amy, appreciating the fact that Nick understood. She knew he was pleased with how they'd treated Dylan – and was sure he was eager to get him back to his stable for further training. If Nick hadn't taken on Storm, Dylan would have returned home last week, but Nick was paying to keep Dylan at Heartland until he was able to arrange an open stall for the young jumper.

"Is everything OK there?" she asked. "No sign of the flu?"

"So far, so good," Nick responded.

"Could I speak to Daniel?" asked Amy. "I'd like to ask him about Storm."

"Of course," said Nick. "I'll call him for you."

While Amy waited for Daniel to come to the phone, she thought again about the argument between Ben and Ty. Ty was usually so calm, so understanding. *The stress is getting to all of us,* Amy thought. Then she heard Daniel's voice. "Hi, Daniel," she said. "I just wanted to check on Storm. I know you don't have the flu there, but I can't help worrying about him."

"Everything's fine," Daniel assured her. "Storm's going as well as ever. We're entered in High Juniors on Saturday. How are things at Heartland?"

"Not so great," admitted Amy. "We have another case of flu."

"That's tough," sympathized Daniel. "I guess that means

Ben and Red are out of action for a while."

"Yes," she agreed. "And Ben's not taking it too well."

"I can imagine," said Daniel. "Red's going so well. It's a shame to lose that momentum."

Amy felt a wave of relief. It was nice to talk to someone who understood the situation. "It's tough on him, I know. But it's creating problems here," she said. "Ty doesn't really understand why a few shows should mean so much to him. He doesn't care if Ben qualifies. He says it's the sick horses that we need to worry about. They had a fight in front of all of us, and I feel caught in the middle."

"Yeah, I guess you can see both points of view," said Daniel thoughtfully. "It's hard when you're stuck in the middle. Sounds like you could use a break. Maybe you should come over and visit Storm. It'd be an excuse to get away."

"That's a good idea," said Amy. "I'll ask Lou if she can bring me over. I miss him."

"I bet you do," said Daniel warmly. "He's a horse in a million."

Amy's heart swelled to hear Daniel praising Storm. "I'll see if I can come over tomorrow," she said. Daniel was right – she needed a break from Heartland. "It will be really good to see you. I'm looking forward to it."

After she hung up the phone, Amy's thoughts seemed a lot clearer. She felt sure that she could help Ben and Ty see each other's point of view.

But as she walked towards the barn, the thought was quickly

driven from her mind. Ty was striding towards her, looking dismayed.

"What's wrong?" Amy asked anxiously.

"Solly's started to cough," said Ty. "I was leading him to the new paddock, but I took him inside instead. I'm just on my way to call Scott."

Amy hurried into the barn to see the yearling. He greeted her with a low nicker, and then his body tensed as he began a series of coughs. Amy could see dark patches of sweat on his coat. So she'd been right in thinking it was unlikely that Willow was infected and not Solly, too.

Ty reappeared in the barn doorway and hurriedly pulled on his overalls. "Scott will be here in half an hour," he said. "I thought he should check on Solly right away."

Amy nodded, remembering what Scott had said about younger horses. As they watched, Solly grunted and lay down, his eyes dull and lifeless. Amy quickly crouched down beside him. "Did you take his temperature?" she asked Ty.

"Yes. It's a hundred and four," said Ty. "He must be wiped out."

"Poor boy," said Amy, stroking his forelock away from his eyes. "I'll give him a few drops of echinacea right away." She thought for a moment. "Garlic's good for the immune system, too. I'll put some in his feed, though he probably won't eat much."

Ty nodded. "It's worth trying," he said. "I think this little guy will need all the help he can get."

* * *

Amy found it difficult to get to sleep that night. She kept mulling over the day's events – the new cases of flu, Ty's criticism of Ben, and her conversation with Daniel. She hadn't had a chance to talk to Ty about Ben; once they had diagnosed Solly, it had completely slipped her mind. Caring for the sick horses was so absorbing that she didn't even have time to think much about Storm, and she realized that no one talked about him around the yard. It was as though everyone had forgotten him. But no matter how busy she was, Amy would never forget him, and Daniel understood that better than anyone.

She hoped someone would be able to take her to see him tomorrow. Amy realized that if she didn't visit him soon, it could be weeks before she had the time again. Candy, Willow and Solly might be just the first of many who contracted the flu – when would she ever find the time?

Amy eventually managed to sleep. It seemed she had barely drifted off before her alarm broke through her dreams. She leaped out of bed, determined to organize her day as efficiently as possible.

"Lou," she said, over breakfast, "would you have half an hour to spare sometime today?"

Lou looked up with a smile. "It sounds like someone wants a ride somewhere. Well, I need to go to the feed store, and we're running out of some of the herbal remedies, too. We've been using up a lot of fenugreek and echinacea, for obvious reasons. Where do you need to go?"

"I want to go see Storm," explained Amy. "Do you think you could take me over there?"

"Why? Is he OK?" asked Lou, looking concerned.

"He's fine," said Amy. "But I haven't seen him for a while, and we don't know how many horses will get sick here. If things get worse, I might not be able to go for ages."

"You're right about that," said Lou. "Well, I guess I could take you there on my way to get feed, but you might have to ask for a ride back from Daniel or someone."

"That's OK. Thanks," said Amy gratefully. "Can we go later this morning? I really want to do a session with Blackjack before I go."

"OK," agreed Lou. "Come and find me when you're ready."

When Amy went out, Ben had just finished mucking out the stalls in the front barn and was pushing a wheelbarrow.

"Hey, Ben," Amy greeted him. "How's it going? Is Red OK?"

"He's fine," said Ben, stopping to talk to her. "He seems perfectly healthy, but our sessions aren't very productive. He has way too much energy since I'm not turning him out with the other horses. He's just not concentrating very well. He's already losing form, and the quarantine just started."

"Well, could you do a longer workout or add an extra session on the flat?" Amy suggested.

"Not really," Ben replied. "The yard work is keeping me busy, with you and Ty giving so much time to the sick horses."

Amy felt a pang of guilt. "I know it's difficult. I'll ask Soraya to come over again," offered Amy. "That'll give you a little more time."

Ben simply shrugged. "Thanks," he said briefly, picking up

the wheelbarrow again and trudging off towards the muck heap. Amy watched him go, feeling slightly annoyed that he couldn't be more gracious about the situation. Soraya was right. Ben was preoccupied. And as much as she didn't want to admit it, Ty was right about Ben being selfish, too.

She went into the feed-room. Blackjack was difficult to catch. It was one of the things they needed to work on, but for the moment Amy wanted to get more of an overall opinion of what was troubling the black show horse. She threw a handful of pony nuts into a bucket and set off for the paddocks.

Blackjack was grazing near the gate. Amy watched him for a few moments. The gelding was fifteen years old and had been a successful show horse for eleven years, competing in barrel races at Western shows. It was strange that he was becoming so difficult to handle as he grew older. Amy instinctively felt that he must be in pain, but he didn't appear to have lost any mobility.

She rattled the bucket, and Blackjack looked up. He stared at Amy for a moment, then returned to grazing. Amy let herself into the paddock and walked towards him slowly, rattling the bucket again. Blackjack stopped grazing once more and walked away more purposefully, turning his back to Amy.

Amy put the bucket down and followed him around the paddock, not trying to catch him but not letting him graze, either. She wanted to get a feel for the horse's character. She watched his eyes as she forced him to keep walking around the paddock. He often rolled them as she got closer, showing the whites, and he flicked his ears back in annoyance. He wasn't afraid, she was sure of that. There was no tension in his body. The only term she could give to his expression was ... resentful. *Leave me alone,* he seemed to be saying. But why?

After Amy followed him for forty minutes, Blackjack finally allowed her to come closer. She moved near him and stroked his neck. Blackjack glared at her, his ears pinned back. *He's so angry,* she thought. She stepped back and allowed him to return to grazing. She'd put some beech and holly flower remedies in his water, she decided. Whatever it was that he resented, the remedies would help counteract his feelings. It would be a start.

Before leaving the paddock, she did a quick inspection of the other horses. They needed to be checked over at least twice a day for signs of flu. To her dismay, Sugarfoot, the little Shetland pony that was a permanent resident at Heartland, had a runny nose and a temperature.

"Oh, Sugarfoot," said Amy when the little pony coughed three times in succession. "Let's get you up to the barn."

Ty was already in the barn, nursing Solly. Neither the yearling nor Willow had improved overnight. Both were still running high temperatures, and Solly's cough had worsened. Ty, looking tired, sighed when he saw Sugarfoot.

"He can go next to Willow," he said. "I'm going to move Solly up a few stalls, away from the door. Scott said it's important to keep them warm and out of draughts, especially the younger ones."

"Let's move Solly into the stall next to Willow," suggested

Amy. "They're so attached to each other. Then we can put Sugarfoot next to Solly."

"That makes sense," agreed Ty. "Not that he cares much about anything just now. He's really miserable. I was going to check Marion's notebooks to see if there's anything else she would have given to ease the symptoms."

It was Amy's mom, Marion, who had set up Heartland and discovered many different ways of treating horses, including herbal remedies and aromatherapy. Both Amy and Ty had learned everything they knew from her before her death the year before.

Amy smiled. "Good idea," she said. "I was going to do that myself. Actually, I'll take a look now – I need to check on our remedy supplies. Lou noticed that we're running low on some of them, and she wants to pick some up when she's out."

Amy went to the feed-room and pulled down Marion's notebooks. She scanned them quickly. *Sage,* she read. *Good for reducing fever. Add small amount of dried herb to feed. Comfrey – excellent for respiratory conditions. Use fresh leaves if available or add 20–30 grams of dried herb to feed.*

She reached the essential oils section. *Peppermint oil can be sprinkled directly on to feed to assist breathing.*

Amy looked along the shelves. There was plenty of dried comfrey, but she would have to ask Lou to get sage and peppermint oil.

"Amy!" called Lou's voice across the yard.

"In here!" replied Amy.

Lou stuck her head around the feed-room door. "Are you ready yet?" she asked. "It's eleven o'clock. I was hoping to be back before lunch."

"Sure," said Amy. "We can go now. I just wanted to make sure we're not running out of anything. Could you add dried sage and peppermint essential oil to your list? They should really help the flu cases."

Amy rushed inside, washed quickly and changed her clothes to make sure she did not infect any of Nick's horses. When she came down the stairs, she could hear Lou's car running. Amy suddenly remembered that she hadn't told Ty about her trip to Nick Halliwell's. She hesitated. Lou was already in the car and impatient to go, and she could just see Ty in the distance, leading Dylan to one of the rings for a much-needed training session. Amy decided she could tell him later and got in beside Lou. *Ty will understand,* she said to herself as they drove down the driveway.

Nick Halliwell's yard was an oasis of tranquility after the tensions of Heartland. Horses were staring out over their half doors, their eyes bright and their ears pricked. One of the working pupils was riding over a course of jumps in a training ring. Amy walked briskly across the gravel courtyard, her spirits lifting at the thought of seeing Storm.

She rounded the corner of a barn aisle, and suddenly Storm's handsome grey head appeared over his stall door. He gave a joyous whinny of recognition. Amy's heart leaped. She ran to Storm and flung her arms around his neck.

"Hello, boy," she whispered. "Have you missed me?"

Storm nuzzled her happily, and she laughed.

"Now, that's a beautiful sight!" said a voice from behind her. Amy spun around. It was Daniel, holding a broom and grinning.

"It's so good to see him," said Amy, smiling back.

"And it's good to see you, too," said Daniel warmly. "How are things at Heartland?"

Amy sighed. "Not great. Four horses have the flu now."

Daniel looked sympathetic. "It would be really awkward if it happened here. Nick said last time his yard had the flu it put training schedules back months. It wrecked his competition plans for an entire season."

"Well, I'm all scrubbed up," said Amy. "No way would I risk spreading it here."

She let herself into Storm's stall and looked him over. "He looks great!" she commented.

"Yeah, Nick's regimen keeps the horses pretty trim," said Daniel. "Storm's got so much energy I can barely keep up with him. Do you want to put him through his paces?"

Amy looked at her friend in surprise. It hadn't occurred to her that she could ride Storm today. But she jumped at the idea. "I'd love to," she said enthusiastically.

Daniel grinned. "I'll go get his tack," he said.

They took Storm to the far training ring, where a course of medium-sized jumps was a permanent fixture. "It's a nice little course," Daniel said. "Storm likes it. He's reached the point where he eats these jumps for breakfast."

"Sounds good," said Amy, laughing, as she swung herself on to the gelding's back. Storm pranced a little as she settled into the saddle, and a familiar thrill went through her. He was such a joy to ride.

"I'll warm him up first," Amy called as she set off at a trot around the ring. Storm's stride was flowing and free, his neck arched as he accepted the bit. He responded willingly when Amy asked him to make circles and figures of eight, his whole body turning around her inside leg. Then she signalled for him to collect his stride, and she could feel the power and control in his muscles as he tucked his hindquarters underneath him.

"Good boy!" she praised him, pushing him into a canter. After a few laps of the training ring, she brought him back to a walk and rode over to Daniel, who was watching at the ringside.

"He's going really well," she said. "I'll take him over some jumps. I was thinking the tyres, the parallel bars, the combination – maybe the yellow upright, and around to the oxer."

Daniel smiled. "He'll fly over those," he said. "You could take him over a couple more, if you wanted."

Amy shook her head. "I'll leave the hard work to you," she said. "I just want to remind myself how he feels."

She turned Storm away from the fence and trotted him in a circle before approaching the first of the jumps. Storm pricked his ears and broke into a canter.

"Easy, boy," murmured Amy, checking him. He sized up the

fence and popped over it easily, flicking up his heels playfully. Amy grinned. This was so much fun. Storm loved showing off, even in the training ring. They sailed around the rest of the jumps, with Storm making them seem totally effortless. Amy trotted him back over to Daniel, clapping him on the neck.

"That was great," she said, sliding off his back. "You're doing a brilliant job with him. He seems so happy."

Their eyes met, and Daniel flushed with pleasure. "Thanks." He opened the gate for her. She led Storm through, and they walked back to the yard together.

"You were right," Amy said. "I really needed a break from Heartland. It's been so stressful over the last few days. Ben's still frustrated. I know it's hard for him, but I don't think he realizes he's being unreasonable."

Daniel smiled. "Always the way with competitive types," he said jokingly. "Wanting to win all the time!"

"Well, I do know how that feels," laughed Amy. Then she grew serious again. "But Ty doesn't, not really. That's what this is all about."

Daniel nodded. "They are pretty different people," he agreed. "But they're both nice guys. They'll work it out between them in time. You shouldn't take it on yourself. It's not your problem."

Amy smiled. "No. You're right. I'll try not to worry, but it's good to be able to talk about it. Thanks, Daniel."

"Anytime," said Daniel. "I just wish you could come over more often."

"So do I," agreed Amy, stroking Storm's neck.

They reached Storm's stall, and Amy undid his girth while Daniel took off his bridle and put on a halter.

"I miss you, Storm," Amy murmured to the grey gelding, resting her head on his strong shoulder for a moment. Then she lifted the saddle off his back. "Where does this go?" she asked.

"I'll take it," said Daniel. He slung the bridle over his shoulder and reached for the saddle. As he took it from Amy, his fingers brushed hers, and he looked into her eyes. "I know what it's like to give up competing, Amy," he said softly. "It's not easy. I really respect you for the choice you've made. I think it took a lot of strength and courage."

Amy was surprised at the intensity in his voice. Daniel hadn't moved, and she stood riveted to the spot, her hand still resting on the saddle. She felt confused, and blushed.

"I…" she began, uncertain what to say.

But Daniel didn't let her say any more. He adjusted his hold of the saddle. And before she realized what was happening, he leaned forward and kissed her.

Chapter Four

Amy felt a rush of shock and bewilderment. She stepped back hurriedly. Daniel stepped back, too, and they stared at each other.

"Daniel – I – sorry…"

"No – I'm sorry," blurted Daniel. "I just…"

Amy swallowed. How had that happened? How had she let it happen? "I'd better get back to Heartland," she said hurriedly, averting her eyes.

"Amy…" began Daniel.

Amy looked up at him, the expression in her eyes beseeching him not to make things worse. He hesitated, then shrugged helplessly. "I can take you back," he said. "I just have to tell Nick."

* * *

The slam of the truck door broke the silence, but Amy could think of nothing to say as Daniel started the engine. The day was turning out hot and humid, and Amy rolled down her window, glad to feel a breeze on her face. She stared out, her eyes on the passing countryside, her mind racing. The sensation of Daniel's kiss still burned on her lips, but the rest of her was numb. She felt terrible. She must somehow have given Daniel the wrong impression, but she had no idea what she might have done.

When they arrived at Heartland, Amy turned to Daniel. "It was good to see Storm," she said awkwardly. She hesitated. He looked at her and gave a tentative nod and then returned to staring out of the front window. "I'll call you soon," she added, and then scrambled out of the pickup before Daniel could say anything.

Rather than going into the farmhouse, Amy hurried across the yard and headed down to the paddock, looking around carefully to make sure she hadn't been seen. She wanted to be alone, to think. She let herself into the far field and walked up to Dylan. He nickered a greeting and ambled over to her, stopping to graze a few feet away.

Amy stepped up to him and stroked his neck, remembering that Nick had first been impressed with Daniel because of his insight with Dylan. Daniel had recognized that Dylan's clumsiness was partly because he was young and that he might develop real talent as a jumper later. Amy had been impressed, too. Daniel was a natural – he could spot talent in horses that everyone else dismissed. Not many people possessed a skill like that.

Still, Amy had known these things before visiting Storm today. She knew she respected Daniel, but something about today was different. Amy thought about their conversation — about Daniel understanding the tension at Heartland, the conflict between Ben and Ty. It was comfortable to talk to someone about the joy of competing and winning, someone who could also put it in perspective. And he knew what she had given up, that Storm was a dream horse, and she had let him go.

Amy couldn't help thinking that Daniel was living a life that could have been hers. She could be a working pupil, if not for Heartland.

But Heartland was too much a part of her, and she couldn't give that up. And Ty cared about Heartland's mission just as much as she did.

With that thought, Amy suddenly remembered how much there was to be done. There were still sick horses, and those that weren't down with the virus needed her attention as well.

She gave Dylan a final pat, but as she did so, the memory of Daniel's kiss flooded back, and she felt her mind fill with a dizzying uncertainty again. She touched her mouth with her fingers and let them linger there. She finally brought her mind back to Heartland and dug her hands in her pockets as she turned away from Dylan and walked to the barn. She wondered if she should tell Ty, if he would understand. The idea that Ty might think she had provoked the kiss haunted her. On the other hand, she would continue to feel terrible if she didn't tell him about it. Maybe it would be better to just be open and have a clear conscience.

Ben's voice pulled her out of her contemplation. "Amy!" he called as she walked towards the farmhouse.

Amy looked around for him and saw that he was just outside Red's stall at the front barn, motioning to her.

"What is it?" she asked, jogging over. As she got closer, she could see that Ben was distraught and immediately guessed what was wrong.

"It's Red," he said. "I think he's coming down with flu. I thought he was just sweating from the heat at first – it's so humid today. But now I don't think so. Can you take a look at him?"

"Of course," said Amy, letting herself into the stall.

She eyed the chestnut gelding. By now, she could recognize the symptoms all too easily. Red's coat was patchy with sweat, and his stance was depressed and dejected. His nose was running, and he was trembling slightly. She looked at Ben, who appeared close to despair.

"I'm sorry, Ben," she said. "It looks like he's caught the virus. But he's so strong. It won't last – he'll be through the worst of it in a few days."

"I know that," said Ben, his voice resigned. "But I won't be able to work him for weeks. It means he's totally out of action. I can't believe it. The show season is over for me."

Amy chose her words carefully. "You're just going to have to change your perspective, Ben," she said gently. "I know it's tough. But you'll have to concentrate on getting him well again and forget about competing for a while."

"Forget?" Ben questioned. "We were so close, Amy. We worked so hard."

Amy shrugged helplessly. "He'll get back in full form. There's still a chance you could qualify, but not if he doesn't get well. We'll need to move him to the back barn," she said. "And I'll make a soft grain mash for him when I do all the others. It'll be easier for him to eat."

Ben seemed completely lost in thought, so Amy slipped Red's halter over his ears and coaxed him forward, opening the stall door. The air was still and heavy, and Red's movements were sluggish. "Come on, boy," she murmured. "Let's get you settled in the back barn. It's cooler there. You'll feel better."

The sound of coughing greeted Amy when she opened the door. With four sick horses already in there, it seemed particularly loud and distressing, and the air was just as thick and stifling as in the front barn. Ty was mucking out Candy's stall and looked up as Amy came into the barn.

"Why didn't you tell me you were going to Nick Halliwell's?" he asked her, wiping the sweat from his forehead.

Amy stared at him, uncertain how to respond to his accusing tone. So much had happened since she had left that morning that she had completely forgotten she hadn't told him. "I — Ty, I'm really sorry. You were busy and Lou was ready to go…" She trailed off.

"We've got four sick horses to look after, Amy," Ty said quietly. "Or five," he corrected himself, looking at Red. "It would have been nice to know you were leaving."

Amy felt her cheeks burning. She wasn't used to Ty lecturing her. "If I hadn't gone today, I might not have had another chance for ages," she burst out defensively. "Everyone around here seems to have forgotten about Storm. I wanted to see him before we had ten sick horses to care for instead of five."

Ty looked surprised. "I'm not saying you shouldn't have gone," he said. "You know I understand that. You just didn't tell me. I didn't even know you were gone."

Why didn't I tell him? Amy asked herself furiously, playing the scene back in her mind. Did it have something to do with Daniel? She tried to think back and remember why she had left so quickly.

"I was going to," she repeated. "I don't know, Ty. It just happened. Lou was in a hurry, the car was running, I – I thought you'd understand."

"Look, it's fine," said Ty, picking up the wheelbarrow. "I'm not going to make a big deal about it. I was going to try to leave early so I could help my mom with some errands, but I called her and told her I'd take care of them tomorrow. There's too much to do here."

Amy thought about what Ty had said. She knew his mom had been dealing with depression for several years and relied on Ty. It was only recently that Ty had agreed to introduce his mom to Amy. He had said that he felt it was time, since Amy was so much a part of his life. Amy thought the meeting had gone well, although Ty's family generally wasn't all that supportive of his work at Heartland.

With so many things going through her mind, Amy felt

confused and guilty. "I was going to prepare the feeds," she said awkwardly, hoping to change the subject. "I'll just make sure Red is comfortable first."

Ty nodded briefly and walked off with the barrow. As he did so, Ben appeared in the doorway, and without changing his boots or putting on overalls, walked straight into the stall where Amy was spreading extra straw for Red.

"Ben, what d'you think you're doing?" Amy demanded. "This is the infected area. You can't just march in here like that. Do you want all the horses to come down with the flu?"

"Seems like they're all coming down with it anyway," Ben retorted.

"You mean Red has, and as far as you're concerned, none of the other horses matter," snapped Amy.

Ben looked at her in astonishment. "You know that's not true," he protested.

"Well, you could start acting like it's not, then," said Amy curtly. "You're so self-centred, seeing the flu as a personal setback. You know, missing a few shows is just missing a few shows. I had to give up my horse – my entire showing career. I have some idea how you are feeling. And I think that if you'd help more with the other horses, it'd take your mind off things with Red and give you another perspective. This isn't easy for any of us, you know."

Ben looked stunned and uncomfortable.

"Red's stall in the front barn needs to be cleaned out and scrubbed down," Amy continued. "Maybe you could do that? I need to start the feeds."

Ben nodded unhappily, and Amy let herself out of Red's new stall. "There are spare overalls and boots in the tack-room," she said over her shoulder. "You'll need to wear them whenever you come in here."

Amy stepped out of the barn and took a deep breath. She was still reeling from what she had said to Ben, but she knew her frustration really stemmed from leftover tension from her discussion with Ty.

She felt slightly shaky and very hot. The afternoon was close and muggy, without a hint of wind. It felt as though a storm might be brewing. Amy suddenly realized that she hadn't eaten since breakfast and decided to get a quick snack before preparing the feeds. It might make her feel better. She headed to the farmhouse.

"Is there any lunch left, Lou?" she asked, looking in the fridge.

Lou was unpacking a box of flower remedies and herbs. "I don't know," she said. "I haven't had anything, either. Can't you just fix something yourself?"

"Fine," Amy responded. "I was just asking."

"Well, I could do without the pointless questions," snapped Lou. "My car overheated on the way back from the store. I just got home. And I have to deal with the finances this afternoon. We can't charge owners for horses that have to stay here longer just to meet the quarantine. And Scott says we won't be OK to release until at least two weeks after the last horse has recovered."

Amy found some leftovers of Grandpa's chicken potpie in the fridge and put them in the microwave.

Lou placed the new bottles and herbs by the door. "Can you take these to the feed-room when you go out?" she asked.

Amy nodded as Lou sat down at the table with a notepad and calculator. "Exactly how many horses are infected now?" Lou asked.

Amy spoke wearily. "Five."

"And how long does the infection last?"

Amy stared at Lou. The tension that had been building up all day was getting the better of her. "Is that all you can think about?" she demanded. "How many days' board we're going to lose?"

Lou's expression was indignant. "No, it is not, Amy," she said in a sarcastic tone. "But if you remember correctly, part of my work here involves making sure that we don't go bankrupt."

"I know that," said Amy. "But we just have to live with this until all the horses are better. A few days won't make that much difference, will they?"

"Of course they'll make a difference," said Lou in an outraged tone.

"Well, what about the money from selling Storm?"

"The payment hasn't come through yet, remember? Listen, our margins are pretty tight. We're not running a summer camp."

"Don't you think I know that?" shouted Amy, her temper finally snapping. "You're blowing things out of proportion, like everyone else around here!"

"Like you're being completely reasonable!" Lou shouted back. "Amy, if anyone's losing—"

"Hey, hey! What's going on?" Grandpa stood at the kitchen door, looking at Amy and Lou in astonishment. "What are you shouting about that can't be discussed in a civilized manner?"

Amy suddenly came to her senses. She and Lou hardly ever argued these days. She passed a hand across her face and sighed. "Sorry, Lou," she said. "I'm just a bit . . . stressed out, between the sick horses and the heat."

"That's OK," said Lou. "I feel the same way. I'm sorry, too."

"Well, that was easy enough," said Grandpa, with a small smile. "The weather forecast did say there might be storms in the area later on today. Maybe that will clear the air."

Amy went outside to find Ty. Usually, when there was a storm, they brought in all the horses, but with the back barn out of bounds, it just wouldn't be possible. She found him hosing down the area in front of the barn. He turned off the hose as she approached.

"Hi," he said quietly.

"Ty," said Amy, "I'm really sorry about earlier. I should have let you know I was going."

Ty smiled at her. "I told you, it's fine," he said. "Forget about it." He held out his hand and pulled her to him. He bent his head to kiss her, and Amy felt a mixture of relief and confusion wash over her. What she and Ty shared felt so right, but she knew she had to tell him about Daniel. She felt her heart beating faster as she looked into his face.

"Ty…" she began.

She stopped as a rumble of thunder sounded overhead. They both looked at the sky. Dark, ugly clouds were beginning to gather, although the air was still hot and oppressive. "It's going to storm," said Ty. "We need to bring in some of the horses."

Amy drew back. "Yes," she said, feeling uncertain. She paused, wondering whether to try to bring up the conversation again. But it was no use. She had missed her chance. The moment had passed. "There isn't enough room in the front barn," she said instead, wiping a bead of sweat from her forehead.

Thunder sounded again, closer this time. "We'll just have to leave the hardier ones," said Ty. "A bit of rain won't hurt them. But we should bring in all the show horses."

Amy nodded. "Dylan, Blackjack," she said, "Duke, Major and Jigsaw. Let's get them all in now."

The horses were all standing huddled together, swishing their tails and looking restless. None of them were grazing. They could clearly sense that a storm was in the air. As Ty approached Major, he leaped aside skittishly with his ears back and then trotted around the paddock with his neck arched and his tail held high.

"I've never seen him act like that before," commented Amy. "Storms sure do weird things to them."

Ty nodded. "I'll get him," he said. "You work on bringing the others in."

Amy walked slowly towards the rest of the horses, not

wanting to alarm them any further. Dylan was standing slightly apart from the others, and she circled around him carefully. He didn't move away as she drew closer, and she was soon able to slip a halter over his head. "Good boy," she said, praising him.

She watched as Ty held out a handful of pony nuts for Major, who was still skittish. The horse was within arm's reach when he bucked and cantered away around the field. Amy decided not to wait for him. She'd get the others in first, then help him if necessary. "Come on, Dylan," she said, giving his lead-rope a tug.

Dylan seemed calmer than the others. He plodded willingly by Amy's side to the gate. She reached for the latch and turned to see how Ty was doing. Just as she did so, Dylan stretched out his neck and coughed.

Chapter Five

Amy stared at Dylan. *Please, please,* she begged silently, *not Dylan.* Quickly, she checked his nostrils. They were still clear. She put her hand on his neck. The horse was perhaps warmer than he should be, but it was a hot afternoon. It was difficult to tell. He wasn't sweating more than usual – yet. But then he coughed again.

"Ty!" she called as Ty at last managed to slip a halter over Major's head. He led the nervous horse over to Amy.

"Not Dylan, too?" he asked, with dread in his voice.

Amy nodded, frowning. "He's coughing," she said. "He doesn't seem to have too many other symptoms. But he doesn't usually cough."

Ty reached out and touched Dylan's nose. "I think we have to assume the worst," he said. "We can put him in the back barn next to Candy."

The sky continued to grumble ominously as Amy headed to the barn with Dylan. She looked up at the clouds, which were gathering into black, angry masses behind the farmhouse. The air hung thick and heavy, but the storm refused to break. Amy wished it would start so that they could get it over with.

She led Dylan into the last stall of the barn, next to Candy, and went to get a thermometer. His temperature wasn't uncomfortably high, but it was above normal, and as she took the reading, he coughed again. There was little doubt that he was infected. Amy covered him with a blanket to make him comfortable, then did a round of the other sick horses. Candy was beginning to eat her hay again, which was a good sign. Willow was following a similar pattern to Candy – her temperature was down one degree, and although she continued to cough, her condition had stabilized. She wasn't getting any worse. Sugarfoot and Red were still in the early stages of infection, so it was difficult to tell how they would cope.

But it was Solly who worried Amy. The yearling looked more dejected than any of the others and was refusing to eat anything, even the soft mashes that Amy prepared every day. His cough was harsh and persistent.

Amy slipped inside his stall and took his temperature. It was still a hundred and four. "I think I need to call Scott out again," she whispered to him, stroking his damp neck. "I hope you're not getting worse. I'll put some molasses and fenugreek in your mash. You'll like that, won't you?" But even as she said it, she knew that Solly was unlikely to eat a single mouthful.

She hurried up to the feed-room, keeping one eye on the sky. A flash of lightning lit up the feed-room door, but the rumble of thunder followed slowly. She got the tub of diluted molasses that they used to dampen the feed. Amy had infused it with cloves of fresh garlic. She poured out some of the mixture, thinking about Solly. Scott's warning about secondary infections worried her. Could the yearling be developing one? *I'll call Scott as soon as I'm done with this,* she said to herself. *And Nick, too.*

But phoning Nick to tell him about Dylan would mean she would risk speaking to Daniel. Her heart thumped in her chest, and her cheeks burned. Why hadn't she told Ty when she had the chance? She'd feel so much better if she had. Now she'd have to wait until they were alone again and, with the storm brewing, that might not be until tomorrow.

Amy quickly headed back to the barn with the feeds and found Ben fussing over Red in his stall. The gelding was pacing around anxiously, despite his flu, and rolling his eyes.

"I don't want to leave him," said Ben. "He hates storms. He's all worked up."

"Sorry, Ben. You know the drill. You have to come to the farmhouse. The storm won't last," said Amy.

This was a policy that Grandpa had set up years ago, when a storm had damaged one of the outbuildings.

"I know, I know," said Ben. "I just wish I could stay with him, that's all." But when Amy had finished distributing the feeds, they headed to the house together. A flash of lightning streaked across their path, almost immediately followed by a loud clap of thunder.

"We're going to get wet!" yelled Ben, breaking into a jog. Amy felt the first heavy drops of rain begin to fall and started to run, too. They piled through the kitchen door as the storm unleashed a true downpour.

Lou was balanced on the kitchen sink, trying to close the window, which already had rain blowing through it.

"I opened it earlier because of the heat," she shouted, yanking at the handle. "Now I can't get it shut."

"Let me try," offered Ben, reaching across the counter to the window.

"Careful, you two!" cautioned Grandpa, coming through from the lounge. "I've just checked all the other windows. We're nice and snug. Where's Ty?"

"He must be in the barn or the paddock," said Amy, heading for the phone. "He'll be in soon. I need to phone Nick Halliwell and Scott. Dylan has the flu, and Solly's getting worse, too."

"I doubt they'll be available in this," said Grandpa, a clap of thunder almost drowning out his voice. "You'd better wait until the storm's blown over."

"Or maybe they're indoors, like us," Amy pointed out. She suddenly realized why she wanted to go ahead and call Nick – she wanted to get it over with before Ty came in. Quickly, she entered the number, her heart pounding.

"Hello, Nick Halliwell's stables," said a voice. She stared at the phone. It was Daniel. As she struggled to think of what to say, Ty came in, his hair plastered over his face from running through the rain and his clothes dripping. She watched as he battled to shut the kitchen door against the gale blowing outside.

"Hello?" Daniel repeated.

"Hi," she managed. "It's Amy."

"Amy," said Daniel. The line crackled, and his voice cut in and out. "Listen, I've been thinking…"

"Sorry, Daniel, I can't really talk right now," said Amy nervously. She didn't want to have to raise her voice, but it was difficult not to with the line being so bad. Out of the corner of her eye, she could see Lou looking at her curiously. "I need to speak with Nick, please," she said loudly.

She struggled to hear Daniel through the hiss of the interference. "… out with the horses … a storm brewing," was all Amy managed to catch. Despite the bad connection, she could hear the frustration in his voice.

"There is here, too," she shouted. "The rain's already started. That must be why the line is breaking up. But I need to tell Nick that Dylan has flu. Could you let him know, please?"

"Sure. I'll tell him. But can't you listen to me for just two sec—"

"Not right now," said Amy urgently. She shot a look around the room. Ty was towelling down his hair, while Ben and Grandpa were still battling with the catch on the kitchen window. Amy could tell that Lou, wiping the rain off the table, was still tuned in to the conversation. "I have to go, OK? I'll speak to you soon." Amy put the phone down hurriedly.

Lou caught her eye and raised an eyebrow. "What was all that about?" she asked. "You're so stressed. Is something going on with Storm?"

Amy felt herself turning bright red. "No – no," she stuttered. Now Ty was looking at her curiously, too. "Nothing's wrong. I just wanted to call Scott before the storm gets any worse. That's all." She smiled self-consciously.

Lou looked sceptical but let it go. "I can call Scott," she said.

Amy handed her the phone and went to the fridge. Her cheeks were still burning, and she didn't want Ty to start asking questions. "Anyone want some iced tea?" she asked over her shoulder, reaching for the pitcher.

"Count me in," said Grandpa.

At that moment, there was a white flash of lightning, followed immediately by an ear-splitting crack of thunder. The sky was getting darker, making the afterglow of the lightning even more dramatic. Then the rain, which had already been heavy, came down in a deluge and lashed against the window.

"Good thing we managed to get that shut!" commented Ben. Everyone gazed out at the storm and listened to the pounding of the rain on the roof, and the crash of one of the old paddock gates slamming open and shut.

"I hope the horses will be OK in the field," said Amy anxiously. "I wish we'd been able to bring them all in."

"They'll be fine," Grandpa reassured her. "They'll pick up their herd instincts and stand together with their backs to the wind. Don't you worry."

Amy stared as dramatic forks of lightning continued to light up the sky. Part of her loved storms and part of her hated them. She found the excitement and the wild beauty of them intriguing somehow, but she knew how much they could disturb the horses. It bothered her that they were out in it, fending for themselves. She hoped Grandpa was right.

She poured some iced tea in the glasses and started to hand them out. She felt calmer now and turned to Ty. "Solly's looking pretty low. I'm worried about him," she said.

Ty nodded. "He's not recovering as well as he should be," he agreed as another blinding flash of lightning sent a blue-white glow over their faces. The thunder, when it followed, seemed to turn into a long growl – a growl that grew and became more persistent.

"What's that?" asked Lou, getting off the phone with Scott.

They all craned their ears. The wind outside seemed to build itself into an even greater fury, and Amy heard branches and debris landing on the roof. The growl outside grew louder. It sounded like a speeding train getting nearer.

Grandpa was suddenly all action. "Everyone into the basement," he instructed. "Now! It's a tornado!"

No one questioned him. They all made their way quickly down the plank steps to the damp, unfurnished room.

"We should all sit down," shouted Grandpa above the noise. "We'll be safest down here. With any luck it'll miss us." He pulled a bunch of towels from the dryer and passed them out for everyone to sit on.

As they settled, the roaring grew. Even with the basement door closed they could hear the windows shake. The wind screamed around the house, whistling through any gaps it could find. Amy held her breath, all her thoughts with the horses outside. Tornadoes were not uncommon in Virginia – Amy had seen them before. But none had come as close to the farm as this. She looked across at Lou. Her sister's face was composed, but her eyes were clearly terrified. Amy realized that this was all totally new to her. Lou had grown up in England, where twisters were extremely rare.

"You OK?" she mouthed over the noise. Lou nodded, hugging her knees. Grandpa put his arm around her.

Amy crept closer to Ty and took his hand. He squeezed it as they listened to the howling winds that rattled around the house. Amy knew that tornadoes could cause phenomenal damage, but she tried to remain calm. As Grandpa said, chances were that it would miss the farm entirely. *But what about the horses in the paddock?* she couldn't help thinking. *What if it hits the barn?*

Just as the noise seemed as though it couldn't get any louder, it suddenly seemed to abate. Amy let out a sigh of relief. Surely the worst was over. But then, from the direction of the barn, there was a distant crashing sound, deeper and more penetrating than the smashing of tiles or twigs that had accompanied the twister's howl.

"The horses!" cried Amy. She couldn't contain herself. She leaped to her feet, ran up the stairs, and dashed through the kitchen to the door. She wasn't thinking about her own safety any more – she just knew she wanted to save the horses from danger. She flung open the door and ran out.

The wind hit her like a punching bag, making her stagger backward. She peered out into the inky gloom. Ty had followed her. He grabbed her arm. "It missed us," he shouted, pointing to a small funnel cloud twisting across distant fields. "It's already breaking up. Let's hope there's not too much damage!"

Amy stared in amazement at the dark, swirling mass. As she watched, it seemed to spin off sideways over the hills, and then it was gone, dissolved into the rest of the storm.

"What was the crashing noise?" cried Amy, peering around the yard. It was strewn with rubbish and twigs, but the stalls themselves looked intact. Above the roar of the wind, Amy could hear the sound of horses whinnying in anxiety and fear. "It's the back barn!" she shouted, pulling Ty by the arm.

Together they battled against the wind and rain and made their way down towards the barn. The light was fading fast, but Amy could still see the silhouette of the building against the grey sky. As they got closer, Amy could hear the shrill whinnies of frightened horses.

"Look!" she screamed. "That branch – it looks like it's smashed through the roof!"

"I'll check on the horses!" cried Ty.

But as he wrenched open the barn door, an arm pulled him back. It was Jack Bartlett. "Don't go in there!" shouted Grandpa. "We don't know if it's safe! I just walked around the back side of the barn. A tree went straight through the roof. It might not be stable."

"But the horses!" protested Ty. "Listen, they're terrified! We have to get them out."

"If they're terrified, they're still alive," insisted Grandpa. "We have to wait. We can't see anything in this mess. The situation will be easier to judge once the storm lifts."

Amy was desperate to check on the horses, but she knew Grandpa was right. She looked at Ty, whose hand was still grasping the barn door latch.

"Back to the house," Jack ordered sternly. "There are a few occasions when the horses have to come second. I know you two aren't capable of seeing that, so I'm making the decision for you. Let's go – now."

Reluctantly, Amy and Ty returned indoors. Amy was shivering. It upset her to hear the horses crying out. Lou handed her a blanket and made her sit down.

"Grandpa's right, Amy," she said, her voice tight. "It's too dangerous to try to do anything in this kind of weather."

Looking into Lou's eyes, Amy could tell what she was thinking. Their mother, Marion, had been killed in a storm while trying to rescue a horse. Amy nodded and wrapped the blanket around herself tightly. Ty turned on the radio, trying to find a weather report, while Lou and Grandpa busied themselves making a light supper.

Ty managed to tune in to a local radio station. "Northern Virginia has been ravaged by violent thunderstorms in the last hour," crackled a voice. "The National Weather Service issued no tornado warnings, but we just received reports of downed power lines and some localized twisters in Stafford, Frederick and Loudon counties. If you have a storm in your area, make sure to take all necessary precautions. Stay tuned for periodic updates."

Amy sat with Ben at the table and sipped a mouthful of hot chicken soup, trying to stay calm. She knew that there was nothing they could do right now. They simply had to wait.

An hour later, the wind had died down, and the rain had slowed. They all put on boots and raincoats, and headed to the yard. It was now completely dark, and the outdoor electricity had been knocked out by the tornado. Everyone carried flashlights. Ben went to check the horses in the fields, while Amy and Ty did a quick check of the horses in the front barn, trying not to frighten them further with the bright flashlight beams. Amy caught glimpses of the whites of their eyes, staring at her apprehensively in the strange light.

Then they headed to the back barn. Grandpa inspected the damage where the tree hit the roof. "It doesn't look as if that tree has moved," he commented. Amy could now see that the tree had been completely torn out of the ground. Its roots were jutting out of the roof. "The gash in the roof looks big, but the structure seems stable. We can see how things look on the inside."

Tentatively, Jack Bartlett pulled open the barn door. The sound roused the horses again. Their high-pitched whinnies filled the air.

"We have to get in there sooner or later," said Amy desperately. "Listen to them."

Grandpa flashed his light around the roof beams. Some damage was visible at the far end where the tree's top limbs had ripped through the corrugated roof, but it didn't look as extensive as it did from the outside. "Well, there doesn't seem to be any immediate danger," he said cautiously.

"Amy and I should go in," said Ty. "The horses know us. They'll be calmer with us."

Grandpa trained his light over the beams one more time, then nodded. "OK," he agreed. "But be very, very careful. If there's any movement at all in the roof, you have to get out immediately. You look out for each other, you hear? I'll try to hook up the back-up generator to get you some light. That'll make everything easier."

Amy and Ty pulled the barn door open further and stepped inside. Amy headed straight for Willow, knowing that the trauma would have affected her the most.

"Hey, girl," Amy called, approaching the pony's stall quietly. Willow recognized her voice and stood stock-still, watching Amy come closer in the dark. Amy reached for the bolt of her stall as Ty flashed his light where the tree had crashed into the roof. The damaged area was at the end, above Candy and Dylan.

"I'll check that nothing's fallen into the stalls," Ty said to Amy, stepping forward slowly. Amy watched and waited, craning her ears for any sound indicating instability. The rain still pattered on the roof and dripped from the damaged beams, the drops shining silver in the rays of the flashlights.

Ty turned his light towards the inside of the stall and trained it on Dylan. The horse was still nervous from the storm, his nostrils flaring and his muscles tense. He snorted at the sudden light and backed up into the corner of his stall. As he did so, a piece of wood fell from the damaged roof and landed on the floor nearby. At that, Dylan shied violently and kicked out hard, hammering the back of the stall with his feet.

"Ty!" screamed Amy, feeling the barn shake. "Come back!"

As Ty hastily took several steps back, Dylan grew more agitated. He circled his stall, eyeing Ty. Ty aimed his flashlight at the roof. After a few minutes of calm, Dylan stood still, giving an occasional choking cough.

"The beams are unstable," said Amy breathlessly. "It sounded like the walls moved when Dylan kicked his stall."

They both stood listening, holding their breath. Above the restless stamping of the horses, Amy heard an unmistakable creak.

"Did you hear that?" she asked Ty nervously.

Ty nodded. "We have to get Dylan and Candy out now. This might be our only chance." He rushed towards Dylan's stall.

Amy watched Ty, hesitating for a split second, then moved towards Candy's stall. Ty slid back the bolt on Dylan's door. The frightened young horse barged forward, slamming his chest against the wooden door. Ty braced himself against the blow in an attempt to restrain Dylan. But the concussion of the blow rattled the old barn. As Amy watched, everything seemed to happen in slow motion.

"No!" she screamed as the beams suddenly gave way, crashing down and engulfing everything she could see. She was flung backward. Everything went black. And then there was nothing.

Chapter Six

The sound of frantic horses echoed dimly, then grew louder. And there were voices. People running, shouting, the sounds fading into a murmur that seemed to be only inside her head. Then there was silence.

Amy opened her eyes. Where was she? What had happened? It seemed so dark and quiet. Then sound returned to her all at once – a rush of noise all around her. She scrambled to her feet, realizing that the whinnies and voices were real. In a flash, she remembered there was a horse needing help and reached for her flashlight, but it didn't work. As her eyes adjusted, she could just make out shapes in the shadows. She felt a dull throb on her forehead and, reaching her hand to her face, found that she was bleeding. Then the barn door burst open and three flashlights blinded her. She shielded her eyes.

"The horse," she croaked. "There's a horse…"

Grandpa and Lou were shining their lights on what lay behind her, their faces rigid with fear. Suddenly, Amy knew that she didn't want to turn around. She didn't want to see. She was stuck in a state of shock. This wasn't real. None of it was real. As long as she didn't look, she could walk away, and everything would be normal again.

But Lou's voice reached her and brought her back. "Amy," Lou was saying urgently. "Amy. What happened? Where's Ty?"

Ty…

"He's with Dylan. He led him out," Amy explained calmly, looking past Lou and Grandpa to try to see outside. "I need to get Candy."

The piercing whinnies penetrated Amy's mind and galvanized her into action. "I have to get Candy," she mumbled to herself. She turned around and stared in disbelief. She couldn't see into Candy's stall. It was blocked by fallen lumber and material from the roof. Next to it, instead of Dylan's stall, there was a twisted pile of beams and rubble.

Suddenly, her voice rose in desperation. "I have to get Candy out!"

She rushed forward and started scrabbling at the rubble. She felt a hand grasp her arm and pull her away.

"Take her to the house," she heard someone saying. "Call the fire department. And we need an ambulance."

The warmth and light of the farmhouse kitchen enveloped Amy as she and Lou stepped through the door. Lou guided her to a chair, and she sank into it while Lou called the emergency services and Scott. Amy realized that she was shaking and her teeth were chattering, but she stayed in the chair, staring straight ahead. Lou seemed to take for ever, dialling and redialling the numbers.

At last she got through. She hung up and quickly found Amy a bottle of lemonade. Then she wrapped a blanket around her and pulled the first-aid kit out of its cupboard. Without speaking, she dipped a cotton ball in antiseptic and started wiping the cut on Amy's forehead.

Amy flinched. The antiseptic stung, but it also helped to clear her mind. As she sat there, everything started coming back.

"Lou…" she began.

"Shhh," said Lou, covering Amy's cut with gauze. "Everything's going to be OK."

"No," said Amy clearly. "It's not OK. Ty's in there. And Dylan. They didn't get out. They're under the roof. It collapsed…"

Lou looked into Amy's eyes. "The fire department will be here as soon as they can. And an ambulance. You're in shock. You should finish your drink."

Obediently, Amy took another swallow and felt a little stronger.

Lou finished dressing her cut and sat down on the chair next to her. "How are you feeling? Can you tell me what happened?" she asked, taking Amy's hands in her own.

Amy took a deep breath. "I remember now." She put a hand

briefly to her forehead and felt the bandage. "Grandpa agreed that Ty and I could go inside to check on the horses while he tried to get the generator working."

Lou nodded. "I was there."

"The horses were all upset. Dylan was really wired. He was right under the damaged part of the roof. Ty headed over to him, and Dylan kicked the back of his stall. That's when we heard the beams creak."

Amy paused, feeling shaky.

"Take your time," said Lou gently.

"I called Ty back, but he just said –" she stopped as tears began to flow – "he said we should get Dylan and Candy out while we had the chance." Amy broke down and sobbed. "I thought he was right. We couldn't leave the horses there, so I headed towards Candy's stall. But then Dylan tried to barge through his stall door, and the beams started to fall, and I don't remember any more."

Lou put her arms around Amy, and Amy buried her head in her sister's shoulder. "It's my fault, Lou," she murmured. "I should have realized. I heard the beams creak."

"It isn't anybody's fault. You couldn't have stopped him. He heard it, too," said Lou, rocking her. "Look, we don't even know what's happened yet. It's difficult to tell in the dark. We have to wait for the fire department."

Amy pulled back from Lou and wiped her face. "I'm going to see what's happening." She stood up, suddenly feeling clearheaded and determined.

Lou hesitated. "Amy, there's nothing to see. You can't

go into that end of the barn."

"I want Ty to know I'm there. He needs to know."

"Amy, you should rest."

But Amy was already halfway to the door. "You don't have to come," she said without looking back.

Lou grabbed a flashlight and followed her sister into the blustery night.

Amy reached the barn to see Ben struggling to hold on to Willow, who was prancing and rearing in a frenzy. Red and Sugarfoot had been tied to railings outside the barn, and Red was straining at the rope with all his strength. His shrill neighs, intensified by the howling wind, spread panic through the other horses. Even mild-mannered Sugarfoot was stamping and flashing the whites of his eyes.

Amy ran directly to Willow. "Hey, girl," she said, trying to keep her voice steady. "Willow, it's me."

Ben looked frazzled. "I can't do anything with her, Amy. Can you take her? Solly's still in the barn. We need to get him outside. The beams are creaking. It feels like the walls are vibrating. There could be more fallout at the far end."

"That's fine," said Amy, taking the lead-rope from him, and Ben plunged into the remains of the barn. She looked around her. There was no sign of Grandpa, but Lou had bravely approached Red, who was almost as frantic as Willow. Through the darkness, Amy could see the horses in the paddock, their shadowy forms huddled together, alert yet unmoving.

Then Amy's gaze fell on the barn. More than anything, she

wanted to follow Ben, to be of more help. She took two determined steps towards the barn door, coaxing Willow on, but the young pony was defiant. Willow threw up her head and planted her hooves, pulling the lead-line taut. Amy tried to urge her on, but Willow would not budge.

"Come on, girl," Amy said, with a tug. Then she glanced back at the pony and realized how wrong she had been. She couldn't risk leading Willow into the barn. Seeing the pony's wild eyes and the tension in her hindquarters, Amy committed herself to doing her best to calm the terrified pony. She needed to focus on what she could really do to help. She started with T-touch, and Willow responded almost immediately. The young mare stopped tearing at the lead-line and threatening to rear, allowing herself to find comfort in Amy's presence. She pricked her ears as Ben appeared at the barn door with Solly.

The yearling was almost rigid with terror, and Ben was coaxing him forward step by step. On seeing her friend, Willow whinnied loudly. Solly called a nervous response and walked forward more willingly.

"Let's get them all away from here," said Ben.

"We can take them up to the front yard," Amy suggested, now realizing that the only thing she could do was care for the horses, to help them feel safe. "Come on, Willow." She led the way with the little pony, who walked close at Amy's side.

"Ben, will you take Red?" called Lou. "He'll be better with you. I can manage Solly."

Amy walked briskly to the front yard. It was only when she got there that she remembered – the front barn was already full. She and Ty had brought in all the show horses. Amy stared at the paddock, her eyes suddenly filling with tears. It seemed an eternity since they had stood together at the gate, examining Dylan and making their decision to take him into the back barn. And now both Ty and Dylan were there.

She turned blindly and led Willow back the way they'd come, rubbing her eyes as she went. "There aren't any empty stalls. We'll have to turn them out," she said abruptly to Ben and Lou, who stared at her in confusion as she came back towards them.

Amy walked Willow rapidly down towards the paddocks. The pony faltered and coughed — she was still sick. Amy slowed down, giving Willow a gentle pat. "I'm sorry, girl," she whispered to the pony. "I wasn't thinking. We'll take it slow."

She took a deep breath as Lou approached, trying to pull herself together.

"Are you OK, Amy?" asked Lou as they turned the horses loose in the field.

"I'm fine," said Amy calmly. "Really, I'll be fine. I should go and get Sugarfoot."

She just wanted to be busy. She wanted to have other things to think about. It was the only way to stop herself from going over the scene again and again in her mind. She wasn't sure she could come to terms with what was happening in the barn right then — or what wasn't happening. There was nothing anyone could do until the fire department arrived. Nothing at all.

Sugarfoot was standing by himself, his back turned to the

wind. Amy's heart went out to the little Shetland. Now that Ben had taken Red away, Sugarfoot was completely composed. Rather than whinnying and crying out in fear, he seemed to be shutting everything out, his head hanging sombrely. As Amy approached, he coughed twice and shifted his weight from one foot to another.

"Come on, boy," said Amy softly, untying him. "Being with the others will cheer you up."

She coaxed the pony forward. His movements were stiff and sluggish, and Amy wished there was a warm stall where she could bed him down. It wasn't going to do any of the sick horses good, being out on a wet night like this, but there wasn't any choice. At least they were all wearing blankets.

After turning Sugarfoot out with the others, Amy stayed by the paddock gate, staring blindly at the dark forms of the horses. She was numb. The only thing she could feel was the throbbing where she had cut her forehead. She closed her eyes. The sound of sirens brought her back to herself, and she looked towards the barn, her heart pounding.

The emergency vehicles were arriving at last. Amy walked back from the paddock, staring at the unearthly glow of the flashing emergency lights on two fire engines and an ambulance. She saw Grandpa and Lou talking to the fire chief. Just as she reached them, the chief turned away and started talking with one of the firefighters.

"What's happening?" she demanded. "Do we know anything?"

"Not yet, honey. They're trying to reach Ty first," said Grandpa. "They have to be careful. He might be safe underneath, but they need to reinforce the roof before they can start the rescue. Otherwise they could dislodge a beam and there could be further damage."

Amy took a deep breath. "What about Dylan? And Candy?"

"Candy is trapped, but they don't think she's hurt," said Grandpa. "We don't know about Dylan. At the moment, they're concentrating on getting Ty free."

Lou reached out and put her arm around Amy. "We just have to wait," she said.

"Isn't there anything I can do?" asked Amy.

"Not really," called the fire chief, overhearing her concern. "To be honest, it would be best if you went to the house. We'll come and tell you when we have any news."

But nobody moved. Everybody just stared at the door of the barn, willing it to open and Ty to walk out. Amy wasn't sure how long they stood there. It felt like hours, the minutes dragging by painfully. Ben joined them after tending to the sick horses in the paddock, and at some point, eventually, so did Scott. Amy stood there, waiting, feeling utterly helpless and lost.

At last, there was a commotion from inside the barn, voices yelling directions. A team of paramedics appeared, carrying a stretcher.

"Ty!" cried Amy. She rushed forward and ran up beside them as they jogged towards the ambulance. Wrapped tightly to the board, Ty was almost completely covered. Amy could only see his face. At that moment, reality struck and Amy was filled with fear.

"Is he alive?" she gasped, trying to grab hold of the stretcher. "Please tell me he's alive."

Chapter Seven

The paramedics pushed past Amy and manoeuvred the stretcher into the ambulance. Amy watched as the medical technicians placed an oxygen mask over Ty's face and attached an IV line to his still body. One of them turned to Amy and gave a brief, non-committal smile.

"He's alive," she said. "Unconscious, but alive." Amy was bewildered to see her start to close the door.

"Excuse me," Jack Bartlett spoke up, attracting the attention of the paramedics as he stepped forward and placed his hands on Amy's shoulders. "Excuse me. My grand-daughter here was also involved in the accident. She was knocked out, a blow to the head. I'd like a doctor to see her."

* * *

Amy was relieved that her grandfather had been able to convince the medics that he needed to ride with her and Ty to Meadowville Park Hospital. It was a nightmarish journey. The vehicle raced down the driveway and out on to the roads, its siren blaring. Amy held her grandfather's hand as she stared out of the back window at the road behind them, strewn with branches and debris from the storm.

They arrived at the hospital within twenty minutes. Ty was rushed inside, while Amy and Grandpa were ushered into a small administration area. The admitting nurse sat them down and produced a form.

"We'll need some personal information," she said. "Are you the next of kin?"

Jack Bartlett shook his head. "No. Ty works with us. But we can give you his parents' number and any basic information you need. And we can answer questions about the accident. Also, I'd like someone to check my granddaughter Amy for a concussion."

"Yes, of course. Let's get the paperwork out of the way first."

Jack Bartlett nodded. Amy sat numbly as he read Ty's full name, date of birth and home address from a card he kept in his wallet. Then the emergency room admitting nurse slid the office window closed as she started to dial Ty's home number. Amy wondered whether she should be making the call herself, if it would be easier for Ty's mom to hear the news from someone she had met, but Grandpa assured her that it was fine to let the nurse take care of it. When the nurse slid the office window open again, she said that Ty's mother would be driving over to the hospital right away.

As Amy waited in the reception area for a doctor to see her, she watched people come in with various injuries from the storm. It was clear that the damage had been widespread.

After the doctor looked at the scrape on her forehead and checked her for complications, Amy headed back to the waiting room to sit with Grandpa. She leaned her head on his shoulder, her mind reeling. *Why didn't I make Ty come back?* she kept thinking. *How could I have let him do it?*

"Are you OK, honey?" Grandpa asked her. "How does your head feel?"

Amy reached up and touched the bandage on her forehead. "It's fine," she said. "It just hurts, and with every throb I keep thinking that I shouldn't have let Ty try to rescue Dylan. I should have told him to just get out."

"Oh, Amy. You can't blame yourself," said Grandpa gently. "It wasn't your fault. You know darn well that Ty is just like you. You are both too stubborn to do anything but what's best for the horses."

Amy sighed heavily. "I've heard you say that before." She knew her grandpa would remember the last time he gave her that kind of advice – after her mother had died.

"That wasn't your fault, either," he reassured her.

Amy sighed heavily. "It seems the worst things never are."

Grandpa put his arm around her, and they lapsed into silence.

* * *

It wasn't long before Amy got restless. She began to feel more and more frightened. What were they doing to Ty? Why didn't they come and speak to her and Grandpa? What if Ty didn't wake up at all? She stood up and began to pace. Wasn't there anything she could do?

Grandpa took his cellphone out of his pocket. "Let's go outside and call Heartland," he suggested. "See how they're coping. They'll be wondering what's happened to us."

Amy nodded, and they headed outside. The night was much quieter now. It was incredible to think that a storm had raged only a few hours earlier. Grandpa handed the phone to Amy, and she dialled Lou's number, hoping she would hear it wherever she was.

"Amy! What's happening?" asked Lou urgently.

"There's no news," Amy told her. "They haven't told us anything except that he's in intensive care. How are things there? Have they got Dylan and Candy out yet?"

Lou's voice became choked. "Oh, Amy, our news isn't any better than yours."

"What?" asked Amy, her heart thudding painfully in her chest. She thought she could hear Lou crying. "What is it?"

"Candy is OK," said Lou in a strangled voice. "They were able to get to her. Ben's turned her out with the others."

"What about Dylan?" asked Amy.

"They got him out in the end. But his left hind leg was totally crushed," said Lou, her voice quavering. "I'm sorry, Amy. There was just no hope for him. Scott had to put him down. It was the only thing he could do."

Amy felt stunned. Dylan, the brave young showjumper that had been at Heartland all summer. Dylan, who was ready to go back to Nick, and who had so much potential. *Ty did so much work with him,* she thought, and the tears began to stream down her cheeks.

"Have you told Nick?" she asked through her tears.

"Not yet," said Lou. "We've been too busy. Ben's worried about the horses that have been turned out and are still sick. He's been putting dry blankets on them. He said Solly is coughing badly. Red and Willow still seem pretty wired, and Willow won't let anyone near her. It's like you're the only person who can calm her."

Amy immediately found herself thinking about the horses — what they would need, where would be the best place to put them, and what she should ask Lou to do. "Throw flakes of hay to the horses in the paddocks," she said. "They haven't had their evening feeds, but that will be enough for tonight." The image of the frightened, sick horses in the dark, wet field came to mind. They needed special care, and Amy felt torn. She knew the horses needed her attention now, especially Willow and Solly. But so did Ty. She needed to know if he was going to be OK. How could she leave him on his own at a time like this?

"Should we do anything special for the horses in the front barn?" Lou questioned. "Should I go ahead and give them their regular feeds? Do they need any supplements?"

Lou trailed off, and Amy made up her mind. "Lou, I'm coming home," she said. "I don't want you and Ben to have to

89

do everything on your own. I'll double-check with the nurse, but it seems like it could be hours before they tell us anything."

"Amy, no," protested Lou. "It's OK. We can cope. You should stay with Ty."

"Ty would want me to come back," said Amy. "He'd understand. It's OK, Lou. Ty's mom is on her way, and I know Grandpa will call us as soon as he hears anything."

Lou was silent for an instant. "Well, if you're sure," she said eventually, and Amy could hear relief in her voice. "Thanks, Amy."

"I'll be home in half an hour," said Amy.

She hung up the phone and turned to Grandpa to tell him the news about Dylan. "I think they need me," she said. "The other horses are still in a state. I want to be here when Ty wakes up, but I have to go now. Will you stay with Ty and let me know if anything happens?"

"Yes," said Grandpa gently. "Ty would want you to go. Don't worry. I'll stay here."

Amy nodded slowly. "Promise you'll call me with any news," she said.

"Of course," said Grandpa. "Come on, let's call you a cab."

Back at Heartland, things were calmer than Amy had expected. Lou ran to meet her and gave her a hug when she stepped out of the car.

"No more news?" Lou whispered.

"Nothing," said Amy, hugging her back.

They walked across the yard, and Lou explained what had

been happening. Ben had turned out five of the healthy horses from the front barn, first covering them all with warm New Zealand blankets. Then he had brought in Sugarfoot, Red and Candy, so they could be warm and dry.

"But he can't catch Willow," Lou explained. "She's gone completely wild again. So he left Solly with her, hoping it'd help calm her down."

"Where's Dylan?" asked Amy.

Lou looked at her. "He's outside the barn," she said softly. "Scott said he would help us take care of the burial tomorrow. He had to make some other calls tonight."

Amy nodded and headed towards the barn. It was important to her to see Dylan. It was the only way to really face what had happened. She saw his still form lying under a tarpaulin, and a lump grew in her throat. Then she stepped forward and crouched down to lift one end of the covering.

She swallowed as she looked down at Dylan's bold, graceful head. Amy reached out and stroked his soft muzzle, which still felt slightly warm. She smiled wistfully as her hand rubbed over the short stubble on his chin. Grief welled up inside her when she realized that Dylan might still be alive if she and Ty had left the barn when they first heard the beams creak. If they had rushed out, Dylan might not have rammed himself into the stall, and the roof might have held until the fire department arrived. Amy knew there were countless possible scenarios, but the reality was that Ty was in the hospital and Dylan was gone.

"Goodbye, Dylan," she whispered, and gently drew the

tarpaulin back over his head. She straightened and headed for the paddock.

The night was now cloudless and beautiful, with a crescent moon and stars shining in the sky. Amy switched off her flashlight as her eyes adjusted to the dark. Most of the horses were dozing, but she quickly spotted Willow and Solly. Willow was standing with her head held high, aware of Amy at the gate. Solly was standing close to her, as if for protection or warmth.

"Willow," called Amy softly.

The bay pony threw her head higher and snorted anxiously.

"Willow, it's me," Amy reassured her. She opened the gate quietly and let herself into the paddock. As she did so, Solly coughed hoarsely, stretching out his neck painfully. Amy approached slowly, not wanting to startle them.

An owl flew overhead with a screech and Willow tensed, ready to flee. Amy stood still, doing nothing. She knew that the trauma of the night could so easily turn Willow back into the nervous, mistrustful pony she had been when she arrived. Amy hoped to break through the layers of fear and delayed shock by providing a calm, reassuring presence.

She wasn't sure how long she stood there, motionless. But all at once she was aware that Willow had taken a step towards her, with Solly still close by her side. Amy waited. Willow took another step, her nostrils flaring.

"Come on, girl," said Amy softly, her heart filling with warmth. Slowly, she held out her hand for the pony to sniff.

Willow stretched out her neck, her breath blowing out in short bursts of fear.

"Good girl," murmured Amy. Willow took one more step, bringing her close enough for Amy to reach up to her neck and touch her. But Amy didn't. Instead, she reached out and stroked Solly, who remained listlessly at Willow's side. Quickly, she clipped a lead-rope to the yearling's halter and began to lead him to the gate.

As she had hoped, Willow's footfalls followed.

Amy settled the two horses into stalls in the front barn. She got some rescue remedy from the feed-room and added it to each horse's water. It would help them all get over their shock. Willow seemed to relax in Amy's presence, and Amy leaned against her warm neck. The pony's response reassured her that she had done the right thing in coming back from the hospital. Heartland needed her now.

She went indoors. "Any news?" she asked.

"Grandpa phoned to say he's on his way home," said Lou. "Ty's mom is at the hospital now."

"But what about Ty?"

Lou shook her head. "There's not much news. Grandpa said the doctors wouldn't say anything."

Amy took this in silently. "What time is it?" she asked. It felt as though the night had lasted a lifetime, and yet she didn't feel tired.

"Half past one," said Lou. She looked pale and exhausted. "Ben's gone home. He says he'll be back first thing to help with the horses. I talked to Nick Halliwell. He's going to send Daniel over to help tomorrow as well."

"Did you tell him about Dylan?" asked Amy.

"Yes. He didn't say much." Lou shrugged. "He was very businesslike. He asked us to arrange for the burial. Since Dylan had been sick, he didn't want to transport him back there."

Amy went to the fridge mechanically. She was hungry, but as she looked at the food on the shelves she knew she couldn't eat any of it. She shut the fridge again and sat down just as Grandpa walked through the door.

Both Amy and Lou rushed to him, and he hugged them both tightly.

"Grandpa, what's going on with Ty?" asked Amy.

Grandpa sighed. "I don't really know," he said. "All they would tell me is that his condition is stable."

"Did you see him?" asked Lou.

Grandpa shook his head. "His mother is there. She'll be the first to see him, I guess. I introduced myself, but it's not the best circumstance for meeting someone. She was having trouble processing everything." He paused and then looked at Amy and Lou. "For now, there's nothing more any of us can do. We should try to get some sleep. Whatever happens, we still have to run this farm tomorrow."

Amy could barely sleep. She lay still, all her muscles tense, ready to jump out of bed at the sound of the phone. But it didn't ring. She thought of Ty's mom. Amy knew she must be alone at the hospital – Ty's dad was out of town.

The hours dragged by, and Amy drifted in and out of a strange, disturbing dream, one in which Ty was riding a horse ahead of her. She was riding Storm and trying to catch up. But however fast she rode, Ty playfully drew away in front. He was always just out of reach.

Amy woke sweating, feeling she had just broken out of a painful struggle. Then the memories of the night before flooded back. She looked at her alarm clock. It was only five-thirty, but the first light of dawn was glimmering outside. She decided to get up.

By daylight, Amy could take in the full havoc wreaked by the storm. The front yard was a total mess, and the back barn was barely recognizable. Amy swallowed as she stared at the gaping hole in the roof, then at the tarpaulin below it on the ground. Ty. Dylan. She turned away, choking back her tears.

I have to check the horses, she told herself. *I have to think about them.* She went to the front barn to see to the sick horses and ponies. First was Red, whose temperature was down despite the desperate night he'd suffered. Candy, too, was much better. Then she came to Solly's stall.

"Solly," called Amy softly, peering over his half door. The yearling was lying down, his nose resting on the bedding. "Hello, boy."

She slid open the bolt. Solly would usually scramble to his feet when she entered the stall, but he stayed where he was. Amy frowned. She stepped past the door and bent down beside him. "Solly!" she whispered urgently. She lifted his head with her hands. "Come on, boy, get up!"

But Solly's eyes were dull and lifeless. His breath was coming in short, rasping gasps, and his neck was dark with sweat.

No, Amy gasped to herself in total dismay. She tried again to get the yearling on his feet, but he lay motionless on the bedding, flopping back each time she lifted his head and neck. It was no use. All her efforts only made his harsh breathing faster and more laboured. *This isn't the flu,* Amy thought. *This is much worse.*

Chapter Eight

Amy sat next to Solly for a moment, gathering her thoughts. This was what Scott had warned them about all along. The problem with the flu wasn't its immediate symptoms. The real danger lay in the infections that followed and the strain the illness put on a horse's heart and lungs. Everything might have been fine if Solly hadn't experienced a night of trauma, half of which was spent out in the damp chill of the storm.

Amy got up and let herself out of the stall. She ran to the house and reached for the phone. When Scott answered sleepily, she realized it was still only six o'clock in the morning, and he must have been up most of the night. But Solly needed him.

"Scott," she blurted into the phone. "Can you come to Heartland? Solly won't get up, and he can hardly breathe. I think he has pneumonia. Please come as soon as possible."

"OK," mumbled Scott. "I'll be right over."

"Thanks," Amy said, breathing a sigh of relief.

She put down the phone. Just as she was about to go back out, she heard the creak of the back stairs. Grandpa came into the kitchen, still wearing his pyjamas.

"What is it, Amy?" he asked. "Did the hospital call?"

"No," said Amy. "It's Solly. I think he's developed pneumonia. Grandpa, I can't get him up. It's so scary. I have to get back to him."

"I'll come with you," said Grandpa, flinging on a coat.

They hurried outside. The sun had now risen and light flooded the yard. Candy and Red put their heads over their half doors. *It's almost as if it's a normal day,* thought Amy. But it was anything but normal.

Solly was still lying down, his chest heaving in stuttered rasps. His eyes rolled as Amy and Grandpa entered the stall. The yearling's distress was apparent in his every movement.

Grandpa nodded gravely. "It does look like pneumonia," he said. He bent down and stroked the young horse's head. "I don't think we should try to lift him, Amy. Let's wait until Scott arrives."

They stayed with Solly, soothing and comforting him, until Scott's shadow fell across the doorway. He let himself into the stall.

"Hi," he greeted Amy and Grandpa quietly. "Solly's not looking so good, is he?"

Scott examined the yearling all over, spending a good deal of time listening to his heart and lungs. "You're right, Amy," he said. "Almost certainly pneumonia. It can be very serious in a horse this young. I was afraid this might happen."

"But will he be OK?" asked Amy.

"He has a good chance of pulling through – with a strong dose of antibiotics," said Scott.

"What other remedies could I try? I don't think I can get him to eat anything. But maybe I could give him a massage with eucalyptus oil, something like that?" asked Amy.

"Yes, that's a good idea," said Scott. "But be sure to keep him warm, and let him rest."

It seemed astonishing that, for the rest of the morning, work at Heartland continued as usual. Amy made a special massage oil with eucalyptus, lavender and rosemary extracts, which would all help Solly's breathing by opening up the nasal passages. By the time she had finished massaging it into the yearling's throat and chest, Ben had arrived and completely swept the front yard. Grandpa had filled all the water buckets, and Lou had finished the morning feeds.

Amy wanted to keep busy. She mucked out all the front stalls, then she checked the horses in the paddock. None of them appeared to have suffered as a result of the storm and, to her relief, none of them showed signs of the flu, either. Amy felt hopeful. It was always possible that no more horses would catch the flu. Surely, Heartland deserved a little bit of good luck now.

She went back up to the yard, planning to spend some time

with Willow. But as she approached her stall, a familiar pickup appeared in the Heartland driveway. Amy's heart dropped. She wasn't ready to deal with this. It was Daniel.

The pickup stopped and he got out. Amy stayed by Willow's stall, uncertain what to do. She brushed the pony's forelock gently but with deliberate focus. She didn't turn away until she heard Daniel's footsteps approach.

"I've come to help," he said quietly.

Amy nodded. "Lou told me you were coming," she said, unable to look him in the eyes.

"Nick told me what you've been through. Amy, I'm so sorry," said Daniel. "About everything. The flu, the storm, Ty … and … and about what happened between us, too."

"No, you don't have to be sorry," said Amy. "It's not your fault. I must have given you the wrong impression. That was such a weird day. Things were so crazy here." She remembered her frustration, her confusion over how to deal with the arguments between Ty and Ben.

"No," said Daniel gently. "That wasn't it. It wasn't just that day."

Amy looked at him curiously. "What do you mean?" she asked, almost afraid to hear the answer.

Daniel met her gaze frankly. "Amy, it's more than that. It's just the person you are."

Amy stared at him. She wasn't sure what to say.

"I mean, you cared so much about Amber and me, even when no one else believed in us. And you didn't give up on me. I wasn't used to having a friend, someone on my side. It was really nice. And now with Storm…" Daniel shrugged, not knowing how to continue. "Anyway, I get that you're with someone else, and I'm sorry," he said, looking into her eyes.

"It's OK," Amy replied, relieved that she didn't have to make some kind of excuse, to try to explain about Ty. She didn't want to have to do that, not now.

"So can we just forget about it?" he asked. "I'm really glad I have you as a friend, and I don't want that to change."

"Yeah," she said. "That sounds good."

"Good," he said, "because I like the fact that I can call you when Storm does well. It's nice to share the news with someone who cares."

"It's nice to hear it, too." Amy offered Daniel a reassuring smile.

He looked around the yard. "But you know, I'm here to help. Just tell me what to do."

Amy sighed, trying to figure out which horses needed attention. "Well, most of the routine stuff is done. You could try doing some work with Blackjack," she said. "He's your kind of horse. He's talented, but his owners say he's been getting more and more stubborn and reluctant. We're trying to figure out why. Maybe you could try grooming him and doing some lunge work. You can see how he is and then let me know if you have any ideas."

"All right," said Daniel. "Leave it to me."

Amy turned back to Willow. The pony was watching her intently from the back of her stall, and the noise of the bolt sliding back made her jump slightly. Amy realized that, after the storm, any sudden noises were bound to frighten her. She fished in her pocket for some alfalfa cubes.

"Hi, Willow," she greeted her, offering them on the palm of her hand. Willow stretched out her neck and blew through her nostrils. Amy knew that her appetite was still low because of the flu and was pleased when the pony lipped up the cubes and chewed them slowly. "Good girl," she whispered.

She put her hand on Willow's neck. The pony still had a slight temperature, but she was over the worst of the virus. And given everything that had happened in the last twenty-four hours, Amy knew it was little short of a miracle that Willow still trusted her.

Amy took a step closer again and began to move her fingers in small, rhythmic T-touch circles, working up Willow's neck. After about ten minutes, she felt the pony's muscles begin to relax. She slowly moved her hands up to the top of Willow's neck. It was good to be doing something so normal, so comforting, something to help her forget what was going on outside the stall.

But she couldn't forget for long. "Amy!" she heard Lou calling. "Where are you?"

Amy's heart immediately thudded in fear. She left the stall as calmly as possible and ran across the yard. "I'm here," she called. "What is it?"

Lou was standing in the farmhouse doorway. "Ty's mom is on the phone," she said. "She wants to speak to you."

Amy rushed inside and grabbed the phone. "Hello, Mrs

Baldwin. Is – is – how is Ty?" asked Amy breathlessly.

"He's out of the intensive care unit," said Mrs Baldwin in a measured tone. "You can come and see him if you'd like."

"So – he's OK?" asked Amy, excitement welling inside her.

There was a long silence, and Amy was puzzled.

"Hello?" she said, thinking perhaps the line had gone dead.

"They – the doctors – aren't sure," Mrs Baldwin managed to say.

"Why?" demanded Amy, a cold chill spilling over her. "What's wrong?"

There was another long silence before Ty's mom spoke again. "They don't know," she said eventually, her voice sounding strained. "It would be easier if you could just come. They'll explain it to you. He's on the third floor."

Amy wondered what was going on and why she wouldn't say more. "OK. I'll be there as soon as I can," she said. "Thanks for calling."

She put the phone down slowly and turned to Lou, feeling alarmed and confused.

"What is it?" asked Lou.

"Ty's mom wants me to go and visit him. There's something wrong, but she wouldn't explain what it is."

"Well," said Lou, "you should go. I'll bet Grandpa can take you. Is there anything I can do here to help out?"

"I'll check on Solly before I go, but someone needs to look in on him every half hour or so and make sure his breathing is regular," Amy explained.

"I can do it," said Lou firmly. "I've got to be outside anyway to organize the feed shipment. And I can sort through the wet blankets for the wash. I'll check on Solly for you."

While Grandpa changed out of his heavy work clothes, Amy went to Solly's stall. She peered over the half door at the little horse. He was still lying down, his chest rising with each shallow breath. Amy let herself in, and Solly raised his head a fraction before letting it sink back down in exhaustion. Amy guessed that the antibiotic injection Scott had given him hadn't taken effect yet.

Amy crouched down by Solly's head and stroked him gently. It seemed hard to believe that only yesterday she and Ty had been discussing how to care for the horses during the storm. Life was so unpredictable, and so fragile – for horses and humans.

She heard Grandpa calling her and stood up. Solly rolled his eyes, almost as though he was begging her to stay, to do whatever she could to make him feel better. "I'm sorry, little one," she whispered to him. "I have to go. I'll be back soon."

All the way to the hospital, Amy tried not to think about what might have happened to Ty. Her imagination kept leaping to conclusions, each worse than the one before. What if his legs had been crushed, and he would never be able to walk again? Or he might have damaged his spinal cord and be paralysed?

What could have happened to make Mrs Baldwin so upset?

Looking out of the car window, Amy suddenly spotted a florist's shop.

"Grandpa, stop," she said. "Wouldn't it be nice to take Ty some flowers?"

Grandpa pulled in, and Amy rushed out of the car. She looked at the sea of colour in front of her and decided she wanted bright, bold flowers. She chose gold and orange gerberas mixed with some yellow roses. *The colours of the sun,* she thought to herself. The man at the counter handed her a small card with a picture of a sunflower on the front to match. Amy pushed the card into her back pocket and hurried to the car.

Grandpa reached out and gave Amy's hand a gentle squeeze. Then he steered the car out of the lot and on to the two-lane highway. Amy smelled the roses' sweet fragrance and thought of how they would make Ty smile.

Grandpa parked in the hospital parking lot, and they made their way inside. Amy gripped the flowers tightly, glad to have something to hold. "We have to go upstairs," she said as they headed for the elevators, "to the third floor."

When they emerged, Amy spotted Ty's mom right away. She was sitting in a waiting area by herself, staring into a plastic coffee cup that she was turning around and around in her hands. Her head and shoulders were bowed. Even without seeing her face, Amy thought she looked tired.

"Mrs Baldwin," said Amy, walking up to her.

Ty's mom looked up. She was pale and she only gave the faintest of smiles. Seeing dark circles under her eyes, Amy guessed she hadn't slept all night.

"This is Jack Bartlett, my grandfather," said Amy.

"Yes. We met last night," said Mrs Baldwin quietly.

"Can we see Ty?" Amy questioned.

"I think it's best if you talk to the doctor first." Mrs Baldwin stood up. "I'll go with you," she said in a soft but brief manner, and began to lead them down a corridor to her right.

Amy's breathing quickened, and her heart fluttered nervously in her chest. Why did they have to see the doctor first? Why was talking to him so important? Amy didn't think it could be good news, not with Mrs Baldwin acting like this.

Mrs Baldwin stopped and talked to a nurse, who nodded and pointed to the doctor's office. They approached the door, and Mrs Baldwin knocked.

Amy quickly scanned the name on the door: Dr Samuel Reubens, Department of Neurology. Neurology? Why would Ty's physician be a neurologist? Before Amy could think it through, she heard someone say, "Come in." They followed Mrs Baldwin through the doorway.

The doctor was younger than Amy had expected, and he motioned for them to come in. Amy felt reassured. Maybe there wasn't too much wrong.

"Please sit down," said Dr Reubens, gesturing towards some chairs.

They sat while the doctor sorted through a pile of papers for a file.

"Mrs Baldwin has asked me to explain Ty's condition to you," said Dr Reubens. "I understand you're his girlfriend."

Amy nodded in response to the doctor, but she thought it sounded awkward for a stranger to be calling her Ty's girlfriend, as if he had some understanding of their relationship.

"And you are?" Dr Reubens looked questioningly at Grandpa.

"I'm Amy's grandfather and the owner of Heartland, where Ty works," said Grandpa.

The doctor opened his file. "As you might expect, Ty suffered extensive injuries as a result of his accident. He has broken his collarbone and his left tibia. That's this bone here," said Dr Reubens, indicating his shin. "There was some internal bleeding as a result of the blow to his abdomen. The emergency room surgeons successfully operated, and the bleeding has stopped. Ty's lower leg is in a cast, and the collarbone fracture will mend in time. He might have to wear a brace, but only temporarily."

Amy let out her breath. So, there was nothing that wouldn't heal.

"With that said, I'm sure you are wondering why you're talking to a neurologist," continued Dr Reubens. He paused and looked frankly at Amy and Grandpa. "I'm afraid the bad news is that Ty also suffered trauma to his head. There must have been a considerable blow, either when the roof collapsed or when he hit the ground. It caused some internal haemorrhaging. He hasn't yet recovered consciousness. To put it simply, he is in a coma."

Amy stared at the doctor. His words sounded strange and unreal.

"A coma?" she repeated blankly.

Dr Reubens nodded. Amy looked across at Grandpa. She was having difficulty taking it all in. Grandpa's expression was stunned, too. She then looked at Mrs Baldwin, who was staring at her hands.

"But ... the coma ..." she stuttered, "how long will it last? When will he wake up?"

The doctor shook his head. "It's impossible to say. The next few days will be crucial. If he pulls through the next week, the chances are good that he'll live. But it could take a lot longer for him to come out of the coma, and we can't be sure if there will be permanent damage."

"You mean..." began Amy.

"We just don't know. As I said, our scans reveal bleeding inside the head, which is the probable cause of the coma. Ty is on medication that encourages the blood flow to return to normal. If he's lucky, he may come out of the coma quickly. And he may have his full faculties, no memory loss or loss of coordination. But the effects of comas are sometimes vast. We can't predict when he will wake up and what the complications might be. It's important that you understand – he may not come out of the coma at all."

Chapter Nine

There was a long silence. Amy and Grandpa both sat still, digesting the news.

"You can visit him if you wish," said Dr Reubens. "I think Mrs Baldwin will be able to show you to his room. Please don't hesitate to come and find me if you have any questions."

Ty's mom, who had remained tense and quiet as the doctor talked to them, stood up and led the way out of the office. In the corridor, Amy didn't know what to say. Mrs Baldwin took a deep breath. "This is a nightmare," she said in a low voice. "I can't believe this is happening."

Amy nodded. "I know," she whispered, but as she looked up, she caught Ty's mother give her a questioning glance. Amy's heart lurched, uncertain how to read Mrs Baldwin's expression.

Amy and Grandpa followed Mrs Baldwin to a room with four beds. To Amy's surprise, three of the beds were empty. There was just one in the corner that had curtains drawn all around it. The nurse pushed the curtains to one side, and Amy gripped Grandpa's arm.

Ty lay on the raised bed, his eyes closed. There were intravenous drips suspended around him, feeding him through tubes, and other machines were reading his vital signs. An electrocardiogram measured his heartbeat with a regular beep. Amy and Grandpa surveyed the scene, overwhelmed by its complexity.

"You can come in and sit down," said a nurse.

Amy drew closer to Ty's bed and placed the flowers on the stand next to him. She stared down at his dear, familiar face. He looked so peaceful, and his breathing was soft and steady. Then Amy turned to Grandpa and buried her face against his chest. He hugged her, and part of her wanted to stay there – to stay turned away so she would not have to see Ty like that any more. The tears streaming down her face gave her an odd sense of comfort.

"We'll leave you for a few moments," Amy heard one of the nurses say.

When the nurses had gone, Ty's mom sat down at his bedside.

After a few minutes, Amy was able to stop her tears and compose herself. Grandpa released her gently, and she turned to look at Ty. He was so pale.

"Ty, can you hear me?" she whispered, not sure what to say.

"It's Amy. Grandpa and I brought you some flowers."

She picked them up and held them in front of his face, as though he might be able to smell them. Then she put them down again and sat in the chair next to his bed. "Everyone at Heartland misses you, Ty," she told him. "We all want you back."

She searched his face for some sign of a response, but there was nothing. After a few moments, there was a bustle of movement outside the curtains and the nurse reappeared.

"Is everything OK here?" the nurse queried, checking on Ty.

"Can he hear us?" Amy asked the nurse. "Can he understand anything at all?"

"It's difficult to know," the nurse replied. "I've known patients who recovered and said they were aware of everything going on around them. Others don't remember a single thing. Even the specialists can't really tell what a coma patient's brain detects. But talking is always a good idea."

"I'll come every day," Amy whispered. "And I'll tell you everything that's going on at Heartland. That way you won't have missed anything when you come back."

Then Amy remembered the card the florist had given her, and she slid it out of her back pocket. She took a pen from her bag and quickly wrote a note: *We all miss you, Ty. But I especially need you. Please get well soon, Amy.*

Amy placed the card next to the flowers and then turned to leave the room.

Mrs Baldwin suddenly gripped Amy's arm. "Did you mean that, what you said earlier, that you'll come every day?" she asked in a low voice. "I don't want to be here on my own. Ty's father is on a business trip, and who knows when he'll be home."

"Of course I'll come," said Amy, feeling a little defensive. Then she added, "But Ty may not be here for that long. He may come out of the coma soon. We have to remember that."

Mrs Baldwin nodded, but as she looked back at her son, she slowly shook her head in disbelief.

Scott's truck was in the driveway when Amy and Grandpa got back to Heartland. Amy jumped out to see why he was there, hoping it wasn't urgent. As she expected, she heard voices coming from Solly's stall and ran to see what was happening.

Both Lou and Scott were bending down over the huddled figure of the yearling.

"How is he?" asked Amy anxiously, leaning over the door.

"Amy!" exclaimed Lou. "You scared me. I didn't hear you. Scott was passing by so he decided to check on Solly. He's pretty much the same. What about Ty? Is he OK?"

Amy met her sister's gaze. She took a deep breath. "He's in a coma."

Scott and Lou stared at Amy in shock. "A coma," repeated Lou. "Did the doctors say when he will wake up?"

"They have no idea. They said it could be tomorrow, or he might never come out of it. Nobody knows."

"Oh, Amy, I'm so sorry," Lou said sympathetically, hugging her sister.

"People do come out of comas," said Scott. "Maybe it doesn't help to say that, but there's still hope…" He trailed off helplessly.

"He broke his leg and collarbone, too," Amy continued. "And they had to operate to stop some internal bleeding. But that's nothing, really, not in comparison."

"How's Ty's mom?" asked Lou as she and Scott let themselves out of Solly's stall. "Is she doing all right?"

Amy thought about Mrs Baldwin's drawn face and tired eyes. She shook her head. "Not really. Ty's dad is away on a trip. I've told her I'll visit every day. I would anyway, but she's so … alone." She then hesitated, wondering if she should continue. "And I can't help but wonder if she thinks the accident was somehow our fault. This must be so hard for her," she said.

Lou smoothed her sister's hair. "Oh, Amy. I don't think she would hold it against us," she said thoughtfully. "At least I hope not. She's probably just trying to make sense of it. It's a lot to deal with, especially on your own." Lou sighed and looked at Amy. "We're lucky we have one another here. It's going to take a lot to hold this place together, and we'll all have to be strong for one another. Come on, Amy," she said, placing her hand on her sister's shoulder. "Let's get something cold to drink. I think we all need one."

Amy nodded. Lou was right. There was so much to do at Heartland, and they would have to keep everything going. Life wasn't going to come to a stop.

"Where's Ben? And Daniel?" she asked. "I should tell them first."

"Daniel's gone," said Lou. "He had to get back to Nick's. I saw Ben with Major, heading towards the training ring."

"I'll find him," said Amy.

She walked past the barn and took the path that led to the training rings. She could see Major trotting around on the lunge line in the smaller ring, with Ben standing in the middle. It was such a normal, everyday Heartland scene, but Amy felt so removed from everything that it seemed as though she were viewing it through a thick wall of glass. She waved at Ben, who brought Major to a halt and led him to the gate.

"How's Ty?" he asked, undoing the latch. "What's the news?"

Amy told him. Ben's face turned white. He seemed lost for words. He played with the lunge line coiled in his hand. Without speaking, he and Amy walked slowly back towards the yard.

"Amy," said Ben suddenly, "there's something I need to say."

"What is it?" asked Amy.

"It's just that – I know I've been selfish lately. With the flu, all I could think about was how many shows I'd miss before Red got well again. I was so frustrated that we wouldn't reach our goal, but I do know that I had my priorities wrong. I mean, Ty pointed it out to me, but I didn't want to admit he was right. I never said I was sorry, and now..."

He stopped, unable to finish the sentence, but Amy knew what he was going to say – "Maybe I won't get the chance." She didn't want to acknowledge it, but she nodded in understanding. There were things she needed to tell Ty, too. About the whole thing with Daniel, for starters.

"I understand how you feel," she said. "But we just have to let all that stuff go. That's not what's important, and feeling guilty isn't going to bring Ty back to us. We're just going to have to work together and get through this."

"I know," said Ben passionately. "I'll do whatever you need me to. I know I can't replace Ty, but I'll work all hours. I don't mind."

"Thanks, Ben," said Amy, her voice trembling. "I appreciate it."

"Well, I mean it," he said simply.

Amy went into the farmhouse. Lou had made lemonade for everyone. Grandpa got up as she came in and poured her a glass. Amy sat down and took a swallow. She felt incredibly tired and realized that she hadn't eaten properly all day – longer, in fact. She hadn't had a normal meal since before the storm.

"What time is it?" she asked.

"About five o'clock," said Scott. He sighed. "I ought to be going. But I'm still worried about Solly. He needs constant attention."

Amy jerked herself out of her tiredness. "I can care for him. It's OK," she said.

"But Amy, you're exhausted," said Grandpa gently.

"And Solly is in a bad way," said Scott. "He's fighting, but it's touch and go. I've given him another injection. Until he shows improvement, he'll need round-the-clock care."

Amy stared at them. "I can give him that," she insisted. She felt suddenly angry and determined. "I have to," she continued. "It isn't his fault he's sick. He just needs some attention, someone to be there to show they care. He's going to be fine."

Grandpa sighed. "I understand why you feel that way," he said. "But we have to think seriously about how we're going to handle everything. I'm going to try to figure out a schedule. We still have the front barn filled with sick horses, and we're not getting much of Heartland's day-to-day work done."

"I just spoke with Ben," said Amy. "He's willing to work extra hours. I know that Soraya will help out if I ask her to. Daniel can come over."

"And I do have some good news," said Scott. "I've checked all the infected horses. Candy is pretty much over the flu now, and Willow and Red are on the mend, too. Sugarfoot and Solly are the only ones that still need high levels of care."

"And there haven't been any new cases for a few days," said Lou. Then she looked anxious. "Sugarfoot isn't likely to get pneumonia, is he?" she asked. Lou was especially attached to the little Shetland, having bonded with him when she first moved to Heartland.

"Well, he's taking longer to get over the virus than the others," said Scott cautiously. "That's probably because he's a little older. Old and young horses are most at risk. But he's strong, and he's being well cared for. He should be OK."

"He won't get pneumonia, Lou," said Amy fiercely. "I'll make sure he doesn't."

Grandpa looked at Amy. "Don't take on too much, Amy. Remember, you promised you'd visit Ty every day as well."

Amy bowed her head. She didn't want anything to keep her from visiting Ty. She needed to be there, but she knew that the horses needed her, too. It was going to be difficult, but they were all her priorities. She was determined. "Grandpa, I want to try. I can care for Solly and Sugarfoot. I just might need help with some of the other work."

"I think Amy's right, Grandpa," said Lou quietly. "If we all stick together, we can get through this."

When Scott had gone, Amy headed back to the front barn. Willow, clearly feeling better, was resting her head over her half door. She whinnied a greeting and Amy smiled. It was good to see the pony's eyes looking bright and calm once more — and a relief that the trauma of the storm didn't seem to have had a lasting effect.

Amy stopped at Sugarfoot's stall and looked in. The little Shetland coughed and shifted restlessly. Amy could tell just from looking at him that his temperature was still high. "I'll groom you after I've taken care of Solly," Amy told him. "That'll make you feel better."

She moved on to Solly's stall. She could hear the unstable breathing of the young horse even before she entered. She decided to make a steam inhalation to help clear his airways and went to the tack-room to get a bucket. She boiled some water and added a few drops of eucalyptus oil, then hurried back to the stall.

"Hi, Solly," she said softly, and crouched down beside him. He was still lying down, and she positioned herself behind his head so that she could offer support. Then she gently lifted his head into her lap.

"Come on, boy," she whispered. "This will make breathing easier for you." She covered his muzzle with a towel and placed the bucket so that the yearling was breathing in the gently medicated steam.

After a minute, Amy noticed that Solly's breathing was deeper and less laboured. "Good boy," she murmured, and as she did so an overwhelming longing washed over her. *If only I knew what to do for Ty,* she thought. In the quietness of the stall, she realized that Ty's absence was beginning to sink in. Her chores, working with the horses, just being in the barn, nothing was the same without him near.

She had been so determined and so strong, telling Grandpa that she could cope. But all at once the reality of what that might mean began to hit her. It meant running Heartland with no one to talk to about the horses, no one who understood the various options for treatment. Instead of discussing the horses' problems with Ty, she would have to deal with them all herself. Ty's ideas were always so insightful, and they worked so well together. Amy had always known that Heartland was close to her, a part of her. But she suddenly realized that so much of what made Heartland fulfilling was sharing the work with Ty. His heart was in the same place as her own, and Heartland could not be the same without him.

Amy buried her head in Solly's mane. "Please get better," she whispered. "Please. You have to..."

Chapter Ten

"Scott's given Candy and Red the all-clear," Amy said, trying to keep her voice light and cheerful. "And Willow, too. He says we can begin to walk them around, but they won't be fully recovered for a few weeks. Ben's just glad that Red's on the mend again. He's been great. He's been working like crazy. He barely goes home. He says he's doing it for you."

Amy paused. "We all are, Ty. We're working so hard to keep things going. I'm looking after Solly and Sugarfoot, and I've started working with Willow again, too. Grandpa's made really good progress on the barn. The insurance ran out last month, and we didn't realize it, so the barn wasn't covered. We're doing as much as we can ourselves. And we've got help from the Carters, the builders from Marlton. They said they'd reconstruct the roof."

She stopped talking, watching Ty's face for some sign of a response. There was none. He had been in a coma for four days now.

"I wonder what you're thinking," she said. She felt as though she should talk the whole time she was there, just in case it might trigger a reaction. "The horses miss you, you know. I think you're Major's favourite. He always looks so hopeful when I go to the paddock. Then he turns away when he sees it's only me.

"Ben and I have been trying to work a little with Blackjack every day. Daniel thought that maybe he was getting stubborn because he felt overworked and taken for granted, so we're trying to give him attention and make him feel appreciated.

"Solly's still fighting his pneumonia. He's had a really bad case. We think it was because he had to be turned out suddenly on the night of the storm. We were afraid that Sugarfoot would get it, too, but it looks like he's pulling through. You know, the doctors told me that pneumonia is the greatest risk to people in a coma. I think of that every time I go to Solly's stall. You have to stay strong, Ty. You have to fight it. Just like Solly, you'll pull through."

Amy heard the curtain being pulled to one side and looked up. It was Ty's mom.

"Hi, Mrs Baldwin," she said.

Ty's mom sat down on a chair beside the bed. "Has there been any change?"

Amy shook her head. "I keep talking to him, though, just in case he can hear."

"I do that, too," Mrs Baldwin said.

They lapsed into silence for a while. Amy had seen Ty's mom a couple of times over the last few days and felt she was beginning to know her a bit better. Mrs Baldwin seemed to react to the situation like any mother would, caught between hopefulness and grief. The thing that struck Amy as odd, though, was that Ty's dad still hadn't come back from his trip. He hadn't visited Ty once.

"Brad's coming back tonight," said Mrs Baldwin suddenly, almost as though she could read Amy's thoughts. She leaned over the bed. "Your dad will be here soon, Ty."

Amy looked at her curiously.

"I know what you must be thinking," she said to Amy, somewhat defensively. "Here's our boy lying in a coma, and his father can't cut short his trip to come back and see him."

Amy smiled awkwardly. She knew that Ty had had issues with his father for a long time. He was a long-distance truck driver, and he hated the idea of Ty working with horses at Heartland. "I guess people have their reasons for what they do," she said.

"I know Brad," Mrs Baldwin said quietly. "He's upset. But whenever something difficult crops up, he buries himself in his work. He sticks to his schedule. It's his way of protecting himself. He hasn't rushed back because he doesn't want to face what's happened. He hopes that by the time he gets here, everything will be OK. That's what he's always done – with me as well."

Amy listened. She wasn't sure what to say. "I – I guess that's one way to deal with it."

Mrs Baldwin's eyes flashed. "Well, it's the only way in our family." Her tone was very matter-of-fact. "You wait around for things to get better. I do it, too. I know Brad isn't fond of Ty's working with horses, so I just don't talk about it. I think maybe it'll pass, or Brad will get used to it."

She played with the rings on her fingers.

Amy thought for a moment. "I'm sure Ty understands why you don't ever bring it up. He doesn't want to upset you. He's really devoted to you."

Mrs Baldwin seemed to consider what Amy had said. "I know he is," she said after a moment. "Ty's the strong one in the family, you know that? He's the one who holds everything together. Don't know what I'd do without him."

Amy reached out for Mrs Baldwin's hand. "It's like that at Heartland, too," she said.

Mrs Baldwin's eyes filled with tears. "Things are going to be different, if he pulls out of this," she said. "I'm going to be there for him. He's never had that. I'll ask him about his job, take a real interest."

It was difficult for Amy, hearing the other side of the story. She'd known that Ty's family life was tough and that he spent a lot of time looking after his mom. But he'd never complained. Not once. He really was the strong one. She turned to look at him.

Her heart nearly stopped. She gasped. Ty's eyes were open.

"Mrs Baldwin!" she exclaimed, turning to Ty's mom in surprise. "Look!"

"What is it?"

Amy pointed, and Ty's mom stared into her son's face. But in the split second that Amy had looked away and turned back to Ty again, his eyes had closed.

"His eyes were open," she stated fiercely. "They were. I swear they were."

"We have to call a nurse," said Mrs Baldwin, standing up suddenly, almost tipping over her chair in agitation. She pushed the call button, jabbing at it repeatedly. Then she gave up and, pushing the curtains aside, rushed to the doorway and shouted down the hall.

"Nurse, nurse!"

A moment later, a nurse appeared and took Mrs Baldwin by the elbow. "What is it?" she asked. "What happened?"

"My son," Mrs Baldwin said breathlessly, rushing towards Ty's bed. "He opened his eyes."

The nurse followed at a measured pace.

"He did," Amy confirmed. "I turned to look at him, and his eyes were wide open. Then – then he must have shut them again."

The nurse shook her head. "Sorry to disappoint you, but I'm afraid that's quite common in coma patients," she said.

She stepped forward and checked Ty's vital signs, noting the readings on the support monitors. Mrs Baldwin watched the nurse's movements closely, trying to gauge her response. Amy waited, desperate to hear that the nurse had been mistaken.

The nurse looked at Mrs Baldwin. "I'm sorry," she said. "There's no change, at least nothing that I can detect now. We'll be taking him for another scan soon, and that will tell us whether there's been any fluctuation in his brain emissions."

"But how?" demanded Amy. "How could he open his eyes like that if he wasn't waking up?"

"It's just a reflex action," the nurse explained. "It has nothing to do with his conscious mind. When people have been in comas for a while, they can have a range of behaviour like that — opening and closing their eyes, making faces. Sometimes they even laugh or cry."

"And it doesn't mean anything?" asked Amy in disbelief.

"No," the nurse said decisively, "it doesn't. I'm really sorry." She smiled. "If it's any comfort, you're doing all the right things. Talking to him, talking to each other by his side. It can all help to bring someone back."

The nurse turned and left the room.

Amy looked over at Mrs Baldwin, wanting to offer her some reassurance. But the woman was not at all aware of Amy. She had taken her seat again by Ty's bedside and was staring at her son's closed eyes.

Amy felt choked with disappointment all the way home on the bus. Every day she got up hoping that Ty would come out of his coma. And every day she had to face the fact that he was still lying in the hospital. Seeing him open his eyes had, in a sense, made everything worse. In the brief moment that she thought she had him back, she realized that it wasn't just talking with Ty about the horses that she missed. It was all the other little things, the things that spoke louder than words could ever do. The way his eyes grew warm when he smiled. The way he pushed his hair back off his forehead. The way he could reassure her and inspire her. The easy way he approached a nervous horse.

Amy wiped a tear away with her sleeve. *I have to be strong,* she reminded herself, knowing she had a lot to do now that she had arrived home. She climbed off the bus and trudged up the Heartland driveway.

Soraya saw her coming and ran to meet her. "Hey," she said, giving her friend a hug. "Is there any change?"

"No," said Amy, and explained how Ty had opened his eyes. "I really thought he was waking up," she finished.

"He will," said Soraya quietly. "We all just have to hang in there until he does." She took Amy's arm. "Hey, come on. I've made a new friend. Let me show you."

She led Amy to Willow's stall in the front barn. The bay pony whinnied a greeting, clearly pleased to see Amy. But then Soraya gently held out her hand and stroked the pony's nose. Willow didn't jump back as she usually did with strangers. She snorted and blew on Soraya's fingers. Seeing Willow's friendliness gave Amy a rush of joy.

"She wouldn't let me do that a few days ago," said Soraya softly. "You've been doing a fantastic job of rebuilding her confidence."

Amy reached up and scratched Willow's neck. "But it's also because you've been here so much, helping out," she said. "She's learned to trust you because of the way you are around her."

Soraya looked delighted and touched at Amy's words. "That's

wonderful. I always love coming to Heartland," she said. "What you do here is so special. It's amazing work to be involved in."

"I don't know," said Amy candidly. "It doesn't feel so amazing right now. I feel like I'm barely making it, like each day is its own struggle."

"It might feel that way now, but it'll get better," Soraya reassured her. "You'll make it through. You're stronger than you'll ever know."

Amy went indoors to find Lou and tell her the latest. She found her in the office holding a letter. To Amy's surprise, her face was flushed, and she looked as though she might have been crying.

"What is it, Lou?" she asked, concerned.

Lou gave a wobbly smile. "Oh, nothing. How's Ty?"

Amy shook her head. "No change. He opened his eyes, but they said it didn't mean anything." When Lou didn't respond, Amy questioned her again. "Are you sure you're OK, Lou? You look upset."

"I'm fine," Lou insisted. "It's just this letter. It's really sweet."

Amy was curious. "What does it say?" she asked.

Lou handed it to her, and Amy scanned the lines, written in a child's handwriting.

Dear Heartland,

My name's Cindy. I'm ten years old, and I'd love to have a pony, only my mom says we don't have room to keep one. I heard what a storm did to Heartland and I was very sad. I'm sending you all my savings because I can't spend them to buy a horse of my own. I hope it helps.

*I've asked my class at school to help, too. We're going to bake cookies
and sell them, then send you the money.*

Lots of love,
Cindy Styal

Amy felt a lump in her throat. She looked up. "How much
did she send?" she asked.

"Twenty-six dollars," said Lou. "It's just so thoughtful of her.
People have been so generous, Amy. I don't know how they
found out. I guess bad news travels fast. Speaking of news
travelling, I should tell you that Dad called, too."

"Dad?"

"He's sending us some money to help fix the barn. He sent
his love to you – and to Ty as well."

"I'll tell him next time I visit," said Amy quietly.

"With Dad's money and the donations people have sent,
we'll be OK financially. The money will cover what we've lost
from the flu outbreak and from our not having storm
insurance."

"Well, at least that's one less thing to worry about," said
Amy. "We'll have Heartland up and running again soon."

Chapter Eleven

"Look, Willow. This is new," said Amy, holding a saddle out for the pony to sniff. Willow nosed the strange object curiously, then turned away. Slowly, so as not to startle her, Amy lifted the saddle on to her back.

"Is that OK, girl?" asked Amy. "Not too scary?"

It certainly seemed OK. Willow's eyes were calm and bright and full of trust in Amy. As Amy moved around to her other side and reached for the girth underneath her belly, the pony snorted and jangled the bit in her mouth.

Willow had been making progress fast. Over the last two days, Amy had succeeded in getting her used to a bridle. More than that, the pony seemed to actually enjoy playing with the gentle snaffle bit in her mouth. Placing a saddle on her back was the next stage in her re-education, and Amy was delighted that Willow was responding to it so well.

Amy buckled the girth loosely, then watched as Willow swung her head around to peer at the saddle. She seemed puzzled but not distressed. She stamped a hind foot and snorted again.

"Let's take you for a little walk," said Amy, untying her lead-rope. "You can see how the saddle and bridle feel together, OK?"

Slowly, she led Willow out of the front yard and down to the smaller training ring. In the larger ring, Ben was riding Red. Amy's heart warmed to see the pair together again. Red had to take it very easy, and Ben wasn't pushing him. It had been a week since Scott had announced that Red was over the infection. Now Ben was able to build on a gentle walk and trot routine, and Red's pleasure at being worked again was clear to see.

Ben waved to Amy as she opened the training ring gate and led Willow inside. She grinned and waved back, then turned to concentrate on the bay pony, who was looking suspiciously at the brightly coloured jumps in the centre of the ring.

"We're not going near those, don't worry," said Amy, leading her around the outside of the ring. "We're just going to see what it feels like to walk around with your tack on."

Willow soon relaxed, happy to follow at Amy's shoulder. The saddle didn't seem to worry her at all. After one round of the ring, Amy stopped and tightened the girth, being careful not to pinch the pony's tender skin. Willow peered around again, uncertain of the new feeling.

"That's it. Take your time," Amy said to the pony. "Take a good look at it."

She knew that the key to a successful backing lay in making sure the pony fully accepted each stage and understood that there was nothing to be afraid of. But Willow seemed far from afraid. She had accepted the saddle without a murmur.

Amy led the pony around one more time, then out of the training ring. "Good girl!" she praised her. "You deserve a good groom after that."

Ben was just finishing his session with Red when Amy led Willow past the other training ring. They walked to the front yard together.

"It's so good to be riding him again," said Ben happily. "I can't believe how much I missed it."

"Has Scott said how long it'll take to get him back to jumping condition?" asked Amy.

"About three weeks," said Ben. "I want to make sure we don't overdo it. It's hard to be patient. Red seems so eager to do more, but I want to follow Scott's guidelines so Red stays well."

Amy smiled appreciatively. Ben's attitude had really changed, she thought. He'd done so much to keep things going since the storm. Heartland would have been lost without him.

"Is that one of the owners?" asked Ben suddenly as a figure walked down the path towards them.

"We're not expecting anyone," said Amy. She stared. It was a woman. Someone she recognized. At first she thought it might be Barbara, Candy's owner. But as the woman came closer, she realized who it was. "It's Ty's mom," she said, amazed. "She didn't say she was coming. Maybe she has news about Ty!"

Amy quickened her stride and waved. Mrs Baldwin stopped. She looked awkward and nervous.

"Hello, Amy," she said uncertainly. "I hope you don't mind me coming."

"Of course not," said Amy anxiously. "Has something happened? Has Ty…"

Amy tried to ignore the stab of disappointment she felt as Ty's mom shook her head.

"No," said Ty's mom. "That's not why I've come. I'm sorry. I – I just wanted to see where my son works."

"That's OK," said Amy, quickly trying to put Mrs Baldwin at ease. She smiled. "It's nice that you came. Do you want to come with me while I put Willow in her stall? Then I can show you around."

Mrs Baldwin nodded and followed Amy to Willow's stall. "I hope I'm not intruding," she began again as Amy unbuckled the pony's girth. "I've just been thinking about you a lot over the last few days. About the way you talk to Ty at the hospital. You seem to have so much to say to him about the horses and what you've been doing with them. You seem to share a lot."

She paused as Amy lifted the saddle off Willow's back and hooked it securely over her arm. Amy was touched by Mrs Baldwin's comment, but she had a feeling that Ty's mom had something else to say, so she waited patiently for her to continue.

Mrs Baldwin looked thoughtful. "Heartland is part of his life," she said, after a moment. "I guess I didn't realize what a big part, but it really matters to him, and I wanted to come and see it for myself."

"I'm glad you came," said Amy as they walked slowly to the tack-room. "I can give you a tour."

After putting Willow's saddle on its rack, she took Mrs Baldwin around to the paddocks, past the feed shed, and to the training rings. When she came to the back barn, she didn't say anything. Mrs Baldwin looked at the structure, taking in the open roof and the new unpainted support beams in silence.

Finally, Amy decided the next stop should be Solly's stall. "The last few weeks have been more than difficult," she explained as she led the way to the front barn. "We had an outbreak of the flu that we were dealing with before the accident. Most of the horses are much better now, but one of our young horses contracted pneumonia. He's in this stall."

They looked over the half door. To Amy's delight, the yearling was standing up and glanced around when he heard them at his door. "His name is Solly," Amy said.

"Here, boy," she called him. She turned to Ty's mom, whose gaze was intent on the yearling. "His cough was awful, and there were days that he was barely able to move, but he's slowly getting better," she said. "We were worried that he wouldn't make it. But I kept telling myself that if we could help Solly pull through, then Ty would make it, too. I know it's silly, but I've been spending almost every waking hour that I wasn't at the hospital here in this stall."

Amy watched encouragingly as the young horse tottered towards her on wobbly legs. "He's still very weak, but he's a whole lot better than he was." She reached down and stroked his neck. "You're going to be OK, aren't you, little one?"

Mrs Baldwin watched in wonder as Solly nibbled at Amy's fingers. "May I pet him?" she asked.

Amy smiled. "Of course," she said. "Come inside the stall. Solly's good with strangers."

She slid back the bolt, and they entered the stall. Amy knelt down beside Solly as he sniffed at Mrs Baldwin curiously.

Ty's mom stroked Solly's forelock for a while. "He's a sweetheart," she murmured. Then, as Mrs Baldwin reached down to pat his neck, Solly reached forward and nibbled lightly at her fingers. Mrs Baldwin looked up at Amy and laughed, and in that moment, Amy realized she and Ty had the same eyes.

"I wish you could see Ty at work here," Amy said. "He is so good with the horses, he knows just how to relate to them. He understands what's important in gaining their trust. He has so much love for what he does…" Amy's voice trailed off.

Mrs Baldwin looked at Amy, her face full of regret. "I should have visited before," she said. "I just didn't understand. There is so much I didn't know."

"It's not too late," said Amy. "It's never too late to understand something new. And you're here now. That's what is important. It's not too late. Ty's coming back. I believe that. Please believe it, too."

Mrs Baldwin nodded. "Yes," she said. "Yes, I hope you're right."

"And I hope you'll come back then, too," Amy said. "It would mean a lot to Ty – and to me."

"Amy! Phone!" called Lou's voice from the farmhouse. "It's Daniel!"

Amy ran across the yard from Candy's stall. She had just finished giving all the horses in the front barn a thorough grooming. Scott had given Heartland the all-clear earlier that day. Since no other horses had contracted the infection, it looked as though they would be able to accept new boarders within a couple of weeks.

Amy grabbed the phone, slightly out of breath. "Daniel?"

"Hi, Amy," said Daniel. "How are things?"

"Not too bad," said Amy. She gave Daniel the update on Ty, telling him that although Ty was still in the coma, he was out of the danger period. They would just have to wait. She also shared the good news that Solly was on the mend.

"That's a relief," said Daniel. "I'm glad he's feeling better. Have you had any luck with Blackjack?"

Amy remembered that Daniel had offered advice on treating Blackjack's bad attitude, but they hadn't had a chance to talk about his progress.

"He seems to be a lot more patient," Amy offered. "Ben and I have been grooming him frequently, and he's been better about being caught in the paddock. He's improving."

"Sounds like it. Well, I guess Ben's happy about the end of the quarantine."

"Of course he is," said Amy. "It'll be a few weeks before he gets back on the circuit, but he's thrilled that Red is getting back into form."

"Well, warn him that he'll have to watch out for new competition," said Daniel, and Amy could detect the excitement in his voice.

"What are you getting at?" Amy asked, already anticipating the news.

"Well, Storm won again today, and Nick was so impressed that he's talking about moving him up to the Intermediate level, because he's just strolling through the High Juniors. So we'll be competing against Ben and Red."

"That's fantastic!" laughed Amy. "Storm will just shine in Intermediate. He's aiming for the stars!"

"There's no doubt about it," said Daniel. "That horse knows he's a winner. You should come and see us."

"I will, when I have a little more time," said Amy, uncertain when that would be. It would be great to see Storm again, but she had other priorities right now.

"Sure," said Daniel. "I hope it won't be long. Say hi to Ty for me next time you go to the hospital. Tell him we're all thinking of him."

"I will," promised Amy. "I'll make sure he knows."

Amy could see the streetlights coming on outside the hospital, one by one. "It's just starting to get dark, Ty," she said to him. "I can see the colours of the sunset through the trees. They're beautiful. You know, it was a really good day. The most amazing thing happened. Your mom came to Heartland. I was so surprised to see her, and she wanted a full tour. It was so nice. We talked about all of the horses you've helped, and she met everyone. I think Major and Solly were her favourites. Solly is slowly getting back to his old self. I told your mom she was invited to come visit any time.

"We have enough money to fix the barn now. Lou's really relieved – you know how Lou likes to keep the finances straight," Amy said with a laugh. "And we'll be able to accept some new horses soon."

Amy looked down at Ty's silent face, remembering what he looked like when he laughed, or smiled, or bent down to kiss her. All the words in the world couldn't replace the hope that was in her heart. "The quarantine is almost over, Ty. But you know it won't be the same without you. Heartland could never be the same. I'm waiting for you, Ty," she whispered fiercely. "We all are. We want you back."

She leaned forward and gave his forehead a kiss. "I need you back."

Wendelin Van Draanen

**Sammy Keyes just can't help it –
if there's a mystery to be solved,
she's sure to find herself right
in the middle of it.**

The award-winning mystery series!

Sammy Keyes
and the
Hotel Thief

Wendelin Van Draanen

SCHOLASTIC

Grams always told her those
binoculars would get her into
trouble. Now Sammy's witnessed
a crime at the Heavenly Hotel — a
light-fingered thief stealing $4000
from Madame Nashira, the astrologer
with the fire-hazard hair-do.
Thing is, while she was watching
him, he was watching her, too...

The award-winning mystery series!

Sammy Keyes
and the
Skeleton Man

Wendelin Van Draanen

SCHOLASTIC

Everyone in Santa Martina knows about
the Bush House. It's big, and dark, and no
one knows who or what's inside. Nobody
with any sense would go there –
especially at Halloween. Except for Sammy
Keyes. And when Sammy goes creeping up
the path, only to be knocked sideways by
a skeleton carrying a bulging pillowcase,
she begins to understand why...